Paul Torday burst on to the literary scene in 2006 with his first novel, *Salmon Fishing in the Yemen*, an immediate international bestseller that has been made into a hit film starring Ewan McGregor, Kristin Scott Thomas and Emily Blunt. His subsequent novels, *The Irresistible Inheritance of Wilberforce*, *The Girl on the Landing*, *The Hopeless Life of Charlie Summers*, *More Than You Can Say*, *The Legacy of Hartlepool Hall* and *Light Shining in the Forest*, were also published to great critical acclaim. He was married with two sons by a previous marriage, had two step-sons and lived close to the River North Tyne. He died at home in December 2013.

By Paul Torday

Salmon Fishing in the Yemen

The Irresistible Inheritance of Wilberforce

The Girl on the Landing

The Hopeless Life of Charlie Summers

More Than You Can Say

The Legacy of Hartlepool Hall

Light Shining in the Forest

Two Eerie Tales of Suspense:
Breakfast at the Hotel Déjà vu and Theo

TWO EERIE TALES
OF SUSPENSE

*Breakfast at the
Hotel Déjà vu*

AND

Theo

PAUL TORDAY

PHOENIX

An Hachette UK company

1 3 5 7 9 10 8 6 4 2

Typeset by GroupFMG using BookCloud

Printed and bound in Great Britain by Clays, St Ives plc

The Orion Publishing Group's policy is to use papers that
are natural, renewable and recyclable products and
made from wood grown in sustainable forests. The logging
and manufacturing processes are expected to conform to
the environmental regulations of the country of origin.

www.orionbooks.co.uk

Breakfast at the Hotel Déjà vu

One

The view from the window of his hotel room was just as he had hoped it would be. Twenty feet below Bobby's window was the decking of a sun terrace. Faded white umbrellas sheltered sets of wooden chairs and round tables. He opened the window and leaned out to obtain a better view. He could glimpse the tops of the heads of a few people who were enjoying the afternoon sunshine, or else sitting in the shade reading newspapers. Beyond the decking, wide stone steps led down into a sort of garden: a garden in the Mediterranean manner, of course, with few flowers and a number of bushes and shrubs dotted around an area of scruffy brown grass. A gravel path meandered through this undistinguished space and then disappeared between two tall cypresses. He knew somehow that this path descended to the rocky seashore and then followed its line around the promontory to the headland. There were no other buildings in sight, just an uninterrupted view of the blue sea.

And what a blue! It reflected an untroubled sky in which the sun was now sinking. There was no wind – at least, there were no whitecaps on the water, just a glassy calm stretching away into the infinite distance. He breathed in, experiencing a sensation of pure pleasure at having arrived here after a tedious journey. There must have been some faint breeze, for he sensed it against his cheeks and, at the same time, became aware of the inimitable fragrance of thyme, and rosemary and myrtle, that he associated with this part of the world.

A faint click made him turn around and he saw that his suitcases had been brought upstairs: discreetly, for he had not been aware of the porter either entering or leaving his room. Well, the man couldn't expect to get a tip if he didn't let people know he was there. Bobby decided that he might as well unpack first, before indulging in any exploration of the hotel. Unpacking was an activity he always enjoyed. He supposed it was some sort of nesting instinct. He hung up his suits in the large oak wardrobe: a beige linen suit to wear on expeditions into the village; a dark-blue suit to wear in the hotel restaurant in case it should be one of those places where people dressed up in the evenings; and a lightweight tweed suit for walking on the rocky hillsides above the hotel. He had read – or someone had told him – that the views were delightful. There was an old monastery, clinging to the side of the mountains, that he believed would repay a visit. Next he set out the leather boxes containing his cufflinks and collar stiffeners, and his set of ivory-backed hairbrushes. In the bathroom he laid out his razor, shaving brushes and various lotions. He had not packed his pillboxes. He had finished with pills. At one point during his illness he had been taking ten different things in the morning and the same again at night. What a bore it had been!

But that was all in the past. The illness that had nearly killed him, the operation that had saved him, and the long and dreary recuperation that followed – all the details had

4

faded from his memory, leaving behind only a sensation of unpleasantness gone by and the hope of better times to come. Now he was as good as new: or rather, he was new, quite new. It was as if he was beginning his life all over again. He was looking forward to a few weeks of absolute rest and quiet, interspersed with some light brain-work: some ideas he was turning over in his mind for a memoir. But it would not be the usual self-congratulatory political biography. He wanted to attempt something more interesting than that.

He folded away his shirts and ties and other garments and placed them in a tallboy that stood next to the ward-robe. Once his unpacking was complete, he stood in the middle of the room and surveyed his new home. It would do. It would definitely do. There was no television or radio to distract him. The bed was large and looked comfortable (he would soon find out if that were true). There was no minibar or any of the other contraptions common to so many hotel rooms: no Internet connection, no electric trouser press. Even the phone was an ordinary phone – an old black handset that must have been installed decades ago – and not one of those contraptions with dozens of buttons and lights that he found so hard to cope with. All in all, the room was . . . civilized. The furniture matched, the faded remnants of gilt and paint suggesting a rather more ornate past, and the room itself was large and light, with Turkish rugs spread over a threadbare carpet. A comfortable armchair, with a reading lamp beside it, sat in one corner and there was a sofa at the end of the bed that looked a convenient place on which to throw his clothes when he undressed at night. A rather grand writing table with a lyre-backed chair stood against one wall: he could easily imagine himself writing not one, but several chapters of his memoir at such a desk. And the bathroom was perfect: a large area of white marble floor surrounding a full-length, cast-iron bath in the centre of the room. The floor might be cold underfoot, but he loved a big bathroom more than anything, and now he had one. The washbasin had brass fittings and marble surrounds. Even the towels were enormous.

He was very glad he had finally made the effort to come here. It had been a project of many years standing. He had long promised himself that, one day, he would cancel all his other engagements, make the journey to the hotel and simply *exist*. He had never managed to do so. There had always been a reason why either he couldn't fit it into his schedule, or else Margaret could not come. Margaret! She should be here with him. It felt wrong that she was not. But if he were honest, just at that moment, he did not really miss her.

How had he first heard about this place? Who had told him about it? He could almost hear the words: 'It's heavenly. Quite unspoiled; marvellous cooking; decent wine list. And the views! The views are to die for.' But maybe it wasn't friends who had told him. He might have read about the hotel in the travel section of one of the Sunday newspapers – except that it didn't seem like the kind of place that had been discovered by the newspapers at all. There were absolutely no concessions to modern life. And it was altogether too quiet for a place that had been 'discovered'.

There was simply nobody about. On the way here, the roads had been empty, the village had looked half asleep and the only shop that was open when the taxi drove past was the pastry shop. That had looked inviting. He would make a point of investigating it on his walk tomorrow. The entrance to the hotel was understated, as if it were simply the drive of someone's house. The car park had been empty, and in the lobby there had been a single person behind the counter, waiting to check him in. The receptionist had been polite, but not effusive, and the formalities of registration had been minimal. He had made the booking some time ago and half wondered if it had ever been confirmed, but the receptionist replied simply, 'Oh yes, we have been expecting you, Mr Wansbeck.' And that was all. He had been shown to his room and handed a large key with a brass fob. Then he was left to himself.

And now what should he do? He had unpacked. The afternoon, or what remained of it, should be used. He thought he should take some exercise before dinner as the fresh air might give him an appetite. At the moment he had none. In truth, he felt rather listless, as if the effort of travelling in trains and taxis had drained him of energy, when all he had done was sit in one seat after another for the last few hours. It felt more like he had journeyed for days rather than hours. Instead of leaving the room, Bobby pulled the chair to the window and looked out at the view.

The brightness of the afternoon was fading into a gentle evening. Strips of cirrus cloud had appeared on the horizon, streaked with gold and red as the sun sank towards the distant horizon. The air was very clear. An inshore wind had started to blow, bending the tops of the cypresses. As day turned to dusk, the sea changed from blue to steel grey, and small waves began to crest and break, streaking the surface with foam. The rock promontory no longer looked inviting but cold and unfriendly. Bobby leaned forward to peer down at the sun terrace below. It was empty. The people he thought he had seen earlier, sunning themselves and reading, had all gone inside. They would be getting ready for dinner, he supposed, having their evening bath and deciding what to wear to the restaurant.

Bobby sat back in his chair and remained motionless for a long while. Far out to sea the dusk gathered, then rolled inland like a dark tide. A single red light like an eye blinked on the horizon – a navigation marker or a light on a fishing boat, Bobby could not tell. It was time for him, too, to think about having a bath and changing for dinner but, just at that moment, the effort seemed too great for him.

'I'll give myself five minutes,' he said aloud. This feeling of inertia was not unknown to him. Ever since his illness, he had been surprised to find that his normal levels of energy would suddenly disappear, as if a tap had been turned off. He knew he would be fine in the morning. The stay would allow him to recharge his batteries and when he returned home his convalescence would at last be over and he would return to his duties with his once-customary vigour. Although, at that moment, he could not think what those duties would be. He had resigned the party whip and stood down as a member of parliament before the last general election. After thirty years of serving his constituency and – he liked to think – his country, he had ceased to exist, at least in a professional sense. And all because of an accounting error, which had been picked up by the *Daily Telegraph*.

Quite a few years ago, Margaret's father had paid off the mortgage on the flat in Chelsea in which they lived when they weren't down in Bobby's constituency. In the first instance, he had provided Margaret and Bobby with the deposit to purchase the flat as a wedding present. Then, a few years later, after some inspired investment on the stock market, he had paid off the balance owed to the building society.

However, Bobby had continued to claim the mortgage interest from the House of Commons Fees Office. He also claimed for the monthly sums of money he paid his wife for secretarial and management services, through a company she had formed for the purpose. In truth, she did very little; Bobby managed most of his own paperwork but Bobby's father-in-law had suggested it would look 'more at arm's length' if the payments appeared to go through a company rather than straight into Margaret's pocket. And Bobby had done no more – or less – than dozens of other colleagues.

Then the *Daily Telegraph* had included his name on a list of other MPs caught up in what became known as the 'expenses scandal', and that was it: his career was over. He had devoted his life to representing his constituents, but that meant nothing to the journalists who wrote about him or to his constituents – and there were many – who read the paper. He had served his country – his *country*, not just his party – with diligence and commitment, but his career had been brought to an end, just to sell a few more copies of a newspaper. At least, that was how it appeared to him. The worst part, or almost the worst, was that the *Telegraph* was the very newspaper that, until that day, had been folded up and placed on the table beside his coffee cup every single morning of his life. He felt as if an old friend had stabbed him in the back.

In Bobby's case, it had all started in the simplest way. He had been having lunch with his father-in-law, Derwent White, who was then an MP himself, and had complained to him about how hard it was to make ends meet. His father-in-law had advised him to use the system to pay himself back a little more in expenses. 'Everyone does it,' Derwent had told him.

But everyone didn't do it, or at least they hadn't been caught doing it.

When the affair – the newspapers called it a 'scandal' – blew up, Bobby's first thought was to travel to his constituency and gather support. He believed he was a popular MP and was liked by his constituents. He thought they would rally behind him and see him through this difficult period. He had not expected the sourness with which he was greeted. His agent wouldn't look him in the eye and one man at a drinks party said, not to his face but well within his hearing, 'I hope these bent politicians rot in hell.'

Then Bobby fell ill. He fell ill and the rest of the scandal, and the general election that followed, passed him by. He wouldn't have been readopted by his constituency anyway, but his illness meant that his constituency never actually had to deselect him. It was a convenient excuse and, after thirty years' service, they simply forgot about him. Now he was out of hospital and unemployed, although, in a way, it didn't matter as much to him as it might have done to other people he could think of. He had achieved a measure of financial independence. He had always been prudent with his money and he felt sure – as sure as one could ever be – that he need feel no anxiety about that aspect of his life. Employed or unemployed, he would never have to

10

worry about where the next meal was coming from. And his needs these days were not great, in any case.

Now, he really must make the effort to get up from this chair by the window and walk through to the bathroom. He pictured himself running a hot bath. He could imagine lying in it, soaking away the stiffness from the journey, relaxing at last and banishing this odd sense of detachment that had overtaken him. Then he would dress and go downstairs and order a whisky and water. He would sit with his drink and people-watch. He and Margaret used to play that game together:

'Oh, that one's a banker, I'm sure of it.'

'Do you think so? I think he looks as if he's just out of prison.'

'*What* is his wife wearing?'

'Do you think she could possibly be his wife? She's years younger than him.'

And so on. There was no Margaret to help him with the guessing game tonight, but it would be interesting to observe his fellow guests. He had no thought of entering into conversation with any of them, not just yet. This place was far enough from home that nobody would recognize him. There would be no awkwardness of that sort: nobody would cut him or, worse, offer him sympathy.

It was just the usual snares of chance acquaintanceship that he had to worry about. The trouble with friendships in a small hotel like this was that they were easy to strike up, but difficult to deal with if they became irksome. He had found, from long experience of staying in hotels or on board cruise ships, that it was best to keep one's distance. He didn't mean to be stand-offish. He just wanted peace and quiet: he would exchange smiles and 'good mornings'

11

with anyone and everyone, but he didn't want to end up sharing a table with complete strangers. He had his own routine and he was going to allow himself the luxury of being quite selfish on this holiday, and sticking to it.

He wondered what the dining room would be like. He had failed to inspect it before he came upstairs. He had a clear picture of it in his mind, however, no doubt as a result of reading the brochure before he made the booking. He pictured a large, airy room, with chandeliers overhead and lots of candles on linen-covered tables. The light would be sparkling off the myriad glasses on the tables: wine glasses with large bowls, champagne flutes, water glasses, crystal decanters dotted here and there. And it would be glinting, too, off the silver tableware, which he had imagined would all be engraved with the crest of the family that had once lived here, before the house became a hotel. It was certainly the sort of place, now that he thought about it, in which guests would wear either suits or evening clothes to dinner, and that meant he would have to change. What a lot of effort just to eat a few mouthfuls, however delicious the food might be, especially when he didn't feel hungry: not at all.

He lay between the clean sheets of his bed, sheets as smooth and flat and cool as marble. He did not even draw the curtains and, from where he lay, he could see a drift of stars across the black sky, like spring flowers emerging from the frozen ground of an unearthly garden. He lay between the clean sheets, not moving, scarcely breathing, and waited for sleep to take him. But it was not so much sleep as a million memories, fragmented and brilliant, that presented themselves to his watchful mind.

12

Two

From his earliest childhood, Bobby had been haunted by a sense of guilt. Other children with such a psychological burden would have dreamed of becoming a superhero, and then grown out of it: not Bobby. Instead, it made him feel he should devote his life to public service.

He and his mother had lived in a cottage on the outskirts of a small village in Bedfordshire. He had dim memories of a larger house, but when he asked his mother about where that house was and when they had lived in it, she only answered, 'This is where we live now, so you had better get used to it.' The house he had once lived in stood like a shadow behind the cottage that was his home for all of his childhood and youth. Behind the cramped little sitting room where they sat, or where Bobby sat and his mother worked her way through piles of documents that never seemed to grow any smaller, was the shadow of a drawing room with a grand piano in one corner and long windows overlooking green lawns. Bobby remembered a nursery too, and the person who came to wake him up every day was not his mother but someone who called herself 'Nanny'. But, over the years, this shadow of another house grew fainter, becoming just a dim, unanswered question in his mind.

His mother worked as secretary to a local school, assisting the board of governors for what must have been a small salary, because life was a struggle. There was nobody else who could help them: both sets of Bobby's grandparents had been killed in bombing raids during the war. The struggle was all the more noticeable because his mother, whatever she might say, had the standards and expectations of someone who had been used to a more luxurious style of living. She would often begin to make some unfavourable comparison, then almost bite off her tongue when she saw how avidly Bobby was listening for clues about his earliest life. She never enlightened him.

Of course Bobby wondered a great deal about who his father was, or had been, and where he was now. He couldn't remember the precise moment in his life when he began to worry about this. As a young child he had accepted the fact. There had been a time when he owned a father, and then there was a time when he no longer had one. He did have a dim memory of the man, but because his mother never spoke about his father, there was nothing on which to nourish this memory and it faded. Whenever he asked his mother about his father, she was dismissive.

'He left us to take our chances a long time ago. I shouldn't worry your head about him, my little man. He's forgotten all about us, *that* I can tell you.'

But Bobby noticed that when his mother spoke like that, it didn't quite ring true. He didn't believe his mother had forgotten all about his father. She sounded like someone who had been wounded, but doesn't like to talk about it. There was a secret behind these words, and a sense of bitterness that she could not quite conceal.

It wasn't until Bobby was in his teens that he began to

14

notice that his mother's bitterness about the past was at the root of the way he felt about himself. She had never been satisfied with him. He was not an especially bright child: his grades were mostly Cs and Bs, never As, and his mother was unimpressed. Praise was rare.

'It simply isn't good enough, Robert,' she would tell him when he showed her the results from whichever exam he had just sat. 'You're not trying.'

His mother was a frail-looking woman, with hair that had always seemed grey to Bobby, although there must have been a time when it was a different colour. Her apparent fragility did not prevent her from voicing her unrelenting determination for Bobby to succeed, however. And he did try; he was trying very hard to succeed. It was simply that he was one of those children who are not especially gifted, either intellectually or physically: a very average boy, in fact. His mother attended all the parent–teacher open days, and even came to watch him on the rare occasions when he played rugby for his school – although there were few such occasions to trouble her. The teachers were afraid of her, and after her visits Bobby always felt that his teachers were picking on him, giving him a hard time because of the hard time his mother had given them.

The question arose as to what Bobby should do with his life. He thought he might become a teacher himself. He might have done well in this profession. By his late teens he had grown into a sturdy, even stout, person of medium height with fair hair and white eyebrows. He had a round pink face and round blue eyes. He looked like someone you could trust, someone dependable. He would look people in the eye when he talked to them

15

and avoided complicated conversations. Consciously or not, he was developing a *persona*. When people met him he wanted them to think: 'He might not have been at the front of the queue when they handed out brains, but he seems a straightforward young man.' And that is what people did begin to think about Bobby, then and later. He recognized his ability to project himself as friendly, uncomplicated, trustworthy.

His mother decided he should read law at university. Bobby still wanted to go to teaching college. He knew he would be good at teaching. He understood exactly how the boys at the back of the classroom felt, struggling to keep up, because he had been one of those boys himself. But his mother told him, 'Your father was a solicitor. Not a very good one. I would like you to be a barrister.'

That was one of the few times his mother mentioned his father. Bobby believed that his father and mother had separated from each other a very long time ago, but he wasn't quite sure how or why they had 'separated', except in the sense that they were apart and not together. Not once had Bobby heard from his father: not a birthday card, not a postal order, not a letter, nor a telephone call. The man might as well not have existed. Perhaps he didn't any more. Bobby was the only absolute evidence that there must once have been a father, for he certainly didn't resemble his mother.

There wasn't a single picture of Bobby's father in the house, not even a wedding photo. When Bobby once found the courage to ask why this was so, his mother told him that when his father had separated himself from her, she had thrown out all of his things. She had purged him as thoroughly as Stalin might one of his rivals. Bobby's father

16

was a non-person. His existence was inferred, rather than a matter of physical proof, just as the existence of a dark star is inferred only by the gravitational disturbance it causes.

The year Bobby was due to go up to university, his mother died. It was not expected, but her health had been poor for so long that it was not a huge surprise either. She had been complaining for a while of headaches and blurred vision, but she was one of those obstinate people who will not go to the doctor's surgery as long as they can still walk or speak. It might not have made any difference if she had gone. She died of a burst blood vessel in her brain. The doctor described her death as being due to 'natural causes'. It was a congenital weakness, he said, and the blood vessel might have burst at any time over the last twenty years.

When she died, Bobby was lost for a while. He missed his mother dreadfully. Although she had been a parent more strict than loving, he had never doubted her love for him. He knew she wanted him to succeed. More than that, after he had been through her effects, he realized why she had been so keen for him to do well.

She had left him some money, not a great deal but enough to see him through university. And she had also left him the cottage, which he decided he would rent out to give himself some extra income. With the help of various friends, he cleared out all the rooms, putting some of his belongings and a few items of his mother's that he wanted to keep into storage, including some pretty bedroom furniture, an old walnut kneehole desk where she had sat and paid her bills and answered correspondence, some pieces of jewellery and a couple of pictures. The rest he had sold or put in a skip.

17

In the desk he found various bills and documents, most of no interest. There were also letters: some that he had written to his mother from boarding school, and an envelope on which he read, in his mother's small, neat handwriting: *To Robert, to be opened in the event of my death.* Inside was a letter dated 30 June 1954. It was not in his mother's hand and was written on plain, cheap-looking paper that had turned yellow with age. It was a letter to his mother. As soon as Bobby read the first few words he knew that, finally, he held in his hands tangible proof of the existence of his father.

Dear Helen,

It is two o'clock in the morning. By the time you read this I shall be long gone. Do not try to follow me. It is best you forget all about me and bring Bobby up as if he had no father. It is best for him that he should never learn about me, and what I have done.

Yesterday at breakfast you saw me open a letter and you noticed, no doubt, that it did not contain good news. You were understandably cross with me when I would not tell you what it was about. The fact is, I couldn't. It was quite beyond me because I am too much of a coward. So I am doing what cowards do: I am writing it all down in a letter, because I cannot tell you to your face.

We have lived well over the last few years, haven't we, my darling? We have a comfortable house, a housekeeper and a gardener. We have a car. We have never wanted for the things we both enjoy in life: good food, the occasional bottle of wine, holidays. You have never asked me how we could manage to do all those things when life is still so difficult for most people, when rationing is only just coming to an end.

Your mother and father would have expected me to provide for you in this way, and I don't regret it. We have had some good times together, haven't we?

But now they must come to an end. The letter I received yesterday was from Andrew Dixon, one of my partners at the office. You might not remember meeting him, but he has been a good friend to me – more than that because he has stuck his neck out for me. Before I left, he told me that Mr Wilson, our senior partner, had employed an auditor to carry out a discreet investigation of our books. Andrew said – without any accusation – that it was thought there was something amiss. I gave him our address here so that he could let me know the outcome of this investigation. And I took other precautions too.

Andrew had written to tell me that they have found out that I have been taking money from a client account – more than one, in fact. I took some money that wasn't mine when we bought the house five years ago. It was from the account of a very wealthy client and the sum I borrowed – I say 'borrowed' because I fully expected to pay it back – was not a large one. But then the lady died and the account formed part of the probate. I was in a panic that I might be discovered and there was no possibility of repaying the money at that moment. So then I had to take money from another account to cover the deficit in the first one. You can imagine how it went on from there. I have been living in the expectation of discovery for years now.

Your husband is a common thief.

If I come home with you, I will certainly be arrested, then sent to prison. The disgrace would kill me and, I dare say, it might kill you too. So I am going to disappear. You need not wonder where to, or what I will do, or how I will live, because I do not know the answers to these questions myself.

I shall not ask you to forgive me. What I have done is unforgivable. I will not excuse myself by saying I did what I did because I wanted a better life than I could otherwise have given you, although that is how it started. That is not how it will end. I know that now.

Do not try to follow me. Forget me. I know you will bring up little Bobby as best you can. Do love him for me too.

With so much love, my darling.

Goodbye,

Philip

Apart from the date, the letter provided no further clues as to where it was written, or what might have happened to its author. So Bobby learned that his father, in his own words, had been a common thief. That he still was a thief, Bobby doubted; it seemed to him that his father must have died long ago, perhaps not long after the letter was sent.

It took Bobby a while to recover his balance after these events, but in the end he did. He found a quality within himself, a toughness, that he hadn't known existed. He also felt a sense of freedom, as if the burden of his mother's expectations had been lifted from his shoulders. All the same, he didn't change his plans.

He went to university in London in 1967 and studied

law, just as she had asked him to do. He managed, with a great effort, to achieve a good enough degree to start him on the road to becoming a barrister. The effort required meant that his social life was not what it might have been. All the same, there was the occasional evening not spent studying and he wasn't by any means a hermit.

Bobby first met Margaret White at a Young Conservatives dance in 1970. Margaret caught his attention in the first place because somebody nudged Bobby's elbow and said: 'That's Margaret White. Her father's loaded.'

Bobby glanced across the room and saw a tall, thin, dark-haired girl with a beaky nose dominating an otherwise attractive face. She was not exactly pretty, but she looked as if she had character. Later in the evening, he made sure his friend introduced them. They talked for a while, then he asked Margaret for a dance. Bobby was not a good dancer, but he didn't tread on her feet or embarrass himself in any other way. Before the evening was over, he had her telephone number and an assurance that she wouldn't mind if he rang her.

It was not love at first sight, but they struck up an acquaintanceship that deepened into friendship over the next two years. He found Margaret to be intelligent, unadventurous and secure in her sense of herself. She had inherited – or learned to imitate – her father's somewhat patrician mannerisms and some people were a little scared of her. Perhaps that was why she was still available at the age of twenty-three, in an era when most people married young. At any rate, she and Bobby got on.

Margaret introduced Bobby to her father, and he became a regular guest at Sunday lunch at the Whites' house in the country, half an hour outside Oxford. Sunday lunch with Margaret's parents and their friends, with a proper roast sirloin of beef and good wine, was something almost unknown to Bobby. The simple meals he had shared with his mother, almost never with anyone else present, had been nothing like this. For the first time, Bobby experienced the pleasures of family life, even if it wasn't his own family.

Margaret's parents took to him too. They liked Bobby: respectful, straightforward, ready to listen. Derwent White liked to talk at his own dining table and he liked young men who nodded and agreed with what he said, which was not always the case with some of the boys that Margaret had brought home. Over time, Derwent and Susan White became almost like a second father and mother to Bobby and it was perhaps as much because of this, rather than any deep passion, that Bobby found himself proposing to Margaret. They were married at St George's Church in Hanover Square in 1972.

It was what everyone expected. It was the right thing to do. They were comfortable in one another's company. Bobby was called to the bar soon after his marriage and found a position in chambers specializing in criminal law.

He had already begun to appreciate that his new father-in-law was a figure of some importance. A merchant banker, and a member of parliament for many years, Derwent White was one of the men behind the throne in the Conservative party. Led by Airey Neave, Derwent White was part of a group within the party that fell out with Edward Heath in 1975 and sought a new leader. Derwent White was one of the unacknowledged kingmakers who helped Margaret Thatcher become leader, and then go on to become prime minister – and the rest, Bobby used to say whenever he told someone else this story in later years, was history.

Derwent White knew many secrets. He knew where the bodies were buried, and he had probably buried a few of them himself. He didn't, by any means, take Bobby into his confidence at first as Bobby wasn't active in politics, although under his father-in-law's influence he was becoming interested in that world. But, eventually, Derwent White dropped enough hints and Bobby fell in love for the first time in his life: he fell in love with the idea of political power, the kind that operates behind the scenes, in small committee rooms and unofficial cabals. He glimpsed a hidden world: one where the real decisions were made, decisions which might change the country's future, and all done over a drink in the members' bar or at one of his father-in-law's clubs.

The secrecy appealed to Bobby. You didn't have to be good-looking, charismatic, or brilliant; you just had to know the right people. The more he thought about it, the more he knew that, above all things, he wanted to be a part of this inner sanctum. He joined his local Conservative party and became active in it. He attended national party conferences at Brighton and Blackpool. He even spoke once or twice and began to be regarded as a useful man.

A short time later, he decided to take the risk of going into politics full time. He wasn't making much money as a junior barrister and he didn't enjoy the work. Politics appealed to him and he sensed a turn in the tide in favour of the Conservative party. His father-in-law had told him that he thought they would be in power for many years, so now was the time to get on board.

Derwent White was influential in the Carlton Club and he ensured that Bobby was listed for a reasonably safe seat. In the general election of 1979, he won that seat and became a member of parliament. His father-in-law was, of course, returned to his seat as well, with an increased majority. At the party Derwent White gave a few days after election night, he handed Bobby a glass of champagne, then patted him on the back. He said: 'You're one of us, now.'

Those words made Bobby happier than anything else anyone else had ever said to him.

Three

The next morning, Bobby awoke to the sound of laughter. A child was giggling somewhere on the terrace below. It was another beautiful day, the sunlight warming the whole room. Bobby wanted to be up and about and doing things. He dressed and went downstairs to breakfast.

As he descended the stairs, a young woman emerged from the dining room followed by a child, a boy of perhaps six years old. The woman was striking. Bobby first glimpsed her in profile and saw an aquiline nose, a chiselled mouth and glossy, shoulder-length brown hair swept back from her forehead. Her complexion was an olive brown and she had an elegant, thin figure. As he watched, she turned her head and said to the boy: 'Don't dawdle or we'll be late.'

So they were English. The woman had spoken with a clear, unaccented diction that gave no clue as to which part of the country she might be from. As she spoke, she gave the boy a look in which irritation and profound love were mixed in equal measure. The boy had stopped, and was gazing up the staircase in Bobby's direction. His look held some indefinable quality that caught Bobby's attention: curiosity, or surprise, or some other emotion he could not quite recognize. Then the boy's mother grabbed his hand and pulled him, firmly but not roughly, in the direction of the hotel entrance, and they went outside.

When he reached the bottom of the stairs, instead of turning left through the double glass doors to the dining room, Bobby walked to the doorway at the front of the hotel and looked out. There was no sign of the woman or boy. They must have been very quick going down the drive or else a car had met them at the entrance, although Bobby had not heard one. He wondered who they were, and whether there were other members of the family staying. He almost thought he might ask the receptionist for their name, but he couldn't see anyone behind the desk, so presumably they were doing paperwork in the back office. Well, it did not matter. If the woman and boy were staying here, he might see them again, and he would say hello – perhaps even introduce himself if the occasion arose.

A little later, he found himself strolling towards the village. He wondered if he might see the woman with her son on his walk, and what it was she was worried about being late for. A bus? The railway station was at least twenty miles from here and the only means of getting there was either by taxi or, he presumed, the occasional local bus. Perhaps they had been going on a picnic or a day trip of some sort and she didn't want to be late for the car that was going to pick them up.

The road to the village was white and dusty. It had once been metalled, but was now covered in loose white gravel, the original tarmac almost wholly disintegrated. It wound up at a gentle gradient away from the sea, between banks of myrtle mingled with sage and juniper, giving off that scent he had smelled last night, a scent that was the

26

essence of this place and the Mediterranean shores. Beyond the roadside banks were stony acres of olive groves, the brown soil interspersed with flakes of limestone. It was a terrain that looked too arid to sustain any form of life, let alone the endless rows of olive trees with their twisted trunks and silvery leaves, but they grew anyway, running up the hillsides until they were too steep for cultivation. Above the groves began a series of limestone ridges populated with holm oak and cypresses and above that, yet more ridges, outlined against the deep-blue sky. Bobby wondered if you could get up there: what mule paths there might be, or other tracks snaking cunningly along the steep hillsides. There must be a way up to the monastery he had seen.

It was not far to the village and, as Bobby approached, he saw a donkey coming towards him from the direction of the main street. It passed without any fuss, taking no notice of him at all, then continued on its journey attended only by a few small flies. He watched the animal until it turned the corner, then resumed his stroll. Now he reached the first houses of the village, almost all lime-washed in either white or terracotta. He heard the distant noise of a radio playing music; he heard the sound of a tractor in the fields; but the main street was empty of people and cars. At the far end was a church – worth a visit perhaps? Now he came to the shops. The first one seemed to specialize only in different kinds of coloured wool, of which balls and strands were displayed behind a dusty windowpane, on shelves covered with dead flies. The shop was closed. Next to that was a shop in whose windows were stacked miscellaneous engine parts such as spark plugs and fan belts. Then Bobby came to the pastry shop he had noticed on the way to the hotel. He could smell it as he drew closer.

The shop was open and a wave of warm air, fragrant with the heady scents of sugar, butter, almonds, honey, apricots and chocolate greeted him as he entered. Inside, a long glass counter ran the full length of the shop. Behind it were shelves full of loaves: white baguettes, focaccia and croissants. Under the glass counter were dozens of different kinds of cake. There were the custard-filled tarts he knew as *pastel de belem*; there was a tray of brioche; another tray of those confections of egg, sugar and almonds that the Spanish call *perrunillas*; *pain au chocolat* and more elaborate cakes too, covered in cream or chocolate icing. Another shelf ran the length of the wall opposite the counter, underneath which there were a few stools, presumably for customers who wanted to eat their cakes on the premises and – yes, there was an espresso machine at the far end, so one could order some of the delicious local coffee to drink as well. Bobby hesitated for a moment and then decided he would indulge himself. Why not? He hadn't eaten any breakfast and now he was hungry. He was definitely hungry. A small selection of cakes and an espresso would hit the spot.

'Hello?' he called. He thought he heard movement and voices coming from the well-lit room at the back where he supposed the bakery ovens were located. Certainly all the warm air seemed to be coming from that direction. There was no reply, which was rather frustrating because he was now absolutely set on having his coffee and cakes and his mouth was salivating – actually salivating – at the thought of them.

'Hello?' he called again, but nobody answered. He stood

28

there for a moment longer, wondering whether he should go behind the counter and look for someone. He wished he hadn't missed breakfast. He had become absorbed in wondering about the young woman and the boy and what had become of them – and had failed to have breakfast, so now he was hungry.

He lingered by the counter, admiring the rows of cakes. He would have one or even two of those little custard-filled tarts, and perhaps a croissant, together with a double espresso and a glass of water. That would be better than breakfast, if only he could persuade someone to come through and serve him. Really, they could scarcely expect any customers with service such as this.

He called again but still nobody came, even though he was certain he could hear movement nearby. Well, he wasn't going to get down on his knees and beg, however tempting the cakes looked – so warm, so fresh from the oven. After a moment he gave up, feeling it would somehow be undignified to wait any longer.

'Very well then,' he said aloud to the empty shop, and left.

Back at the hotel, he found that his room had already been made up. He sat in the chair by the window and looked at the view for a while. This, at least, did not disappoint. There were people on the sun terrace again and he thought he might join them later. He wondered if he might see the young woman and her son there. He was curious to know if she had a husband, or other children, but he could not spot them – just people in sun hats, half hidden by umbrellas or the folds of a newspaper. He would go downstairs in a minute and enjoy an hour of sunshine before lunch.

As he had expected, he felt more energetic this morning. A good sleep the night before had helped him recover from the journey. He decided he might as well see if he could make a few notes for his proposed memoir before he abandoned himself to one of the sun loungers. He would attempt a few opening words, try to capture the tone he wanted, and perhaps sketch out a chapter plan. He knew he had brought a notebook with him and found it in a pocket of one of his suitcases. He drew out the black leather book and opened it. The paper was a smooth, creamy stock that was a pleasure to touch. He found his fountain pen, unscrewed the top and scribbled for a moment on a sheet of hotel notepaper until the ink flowed properly. Then he pulled up his chair to the writing table and sucked the top of his pen (a habit he had retained from his schooldays) before writing the words: *Thirty Years in Parliament*. Underneath he added: *A memoir, by Robert Wansbeck*.

He was certainly not going to write some kind of mea culpa – he was proud of what he had achieved over the last thirty years and he thought other people would be interested too. Of course, he had never been in the front rank of politics, but that, he thought, made his proposed memoir all the more interesting. There were plenty of political autobiographies about. Prime ministers seemed to be able to produce them within minutes of leaving office. Even the people in the Press Office produced books about their time in Downing Street, full of references to the great and the good they had shaken hands with, been photographed with, or had quarrelled with. But what about the poor bloody infantry? That's all he had been: a footslogger. He would write about life in the trenches: the sometimes boring, but always important, work of the average backbencher. He had no doubt his readers would find an account of his life as fascinating as any other politician's, perhaps more so. It was the way you told it.

Bobby started to write and, as he did so, the memories flooded into his mind. Memory: what a wonderful gift that was, and was its absence not the greatest distress that could befall a human being?

When he looked up from the page in front of him, it seemed to Bobby that he had been sitting there for some time, writing. Indeed, he must have done so because both his stomach and his watch told him that the hour for lunch had somehow come and gone. He was quite annoyed with himself. He had been looking forward to a glass of white wine and some seafood – they were sure to have fish or shellfish on the menu in a place like this, right by the sea – and now he had missed lunch. Of course he could order something from room service, but he felt diffident about doing that. It was a small hotel with not many staff and asking them to bring him lunch in the middle of the afternoon would certainly inconvenience someone.

He looked down at the page in the notebook and saw that it was blank. Next to the notebook was a piece of paper with some squiggles of black ink on it, but the front page of the book was still blank. There was not even the title he was quite sure he had written down. He picked up the notebook and turned it over, looking at the back in case he had somehow begun writing at the other end, but that page too was blank. He could not account for it. He must have been dreaming that he had been writing. Perhaps he was more tired from the journey than he realized. For a moment he felt a sense of frustration bordering on anger. Really, he must get a grip on himself.

He went downstairs. Of course it was now the siesta hour and there was nobody about. The reception area had been abandoned to its fate. God help anyone who wanted to check in at this time of day, Bobby thought. He walked past the dining room and along the corridor he thought might lead out directly to the sun terrace. It did. Outside there were half a dozen round wooden tables with parasols, and another dozen sun loungers. A few empty coffee cups and wine glasses stood on the tables, not yet cleared away by the staff – who must be less diligent than he had first thought – but otherwise the place was empty. Someone had left a newspaper on a sun lounger, weighted down with a glass ashtray. A book lay spreadeagled on top of a towel. Everyone must have gone inside to avoid the worst of the afternoon heat.

And it was hot. As he stood there, wondering whether to continue his walk through the sparse garden and along the little path he thought might wind along the headland, he became conscious of a faint dizziness, as if even this brief exposure to the mid-afternoon sun might be too much for him. Perhaps he was a little dehydrated. He could not remember the last time he had drunk anything and his mouth felt dry – the power of suggestion, since he had not been particularly thirsty a moment before. He looked up at the sky and saw the sun burning there in a white glare. Half blinded for an instant, he lowered his gaze and waited for a moment until he could see clearly again, then he walked towards the double glass doors that linked the dining room to the sun terrace to see if he could find a waiter to bring him an iced drink.

As he approached the doors, he could see that just inside was a table on which sat an array of glass tumblers and an enormous jug full of a cloudy liquid. On closer inspection he decided this must be lemonade, because there were slices of lemon and lumps of ice floating in it: exactly what was required. He turned the handle of the door but found it would not open. Some fool had locked it. But why? He could think of no good reason. It must have been locked by accident – perhaps a catch had slipped. He rattled the door, but it remained fast and nobody came to investigate the noise.

He lay between the clean sheets of his bed, sheets smooth and flat and cool as marble. Sleep did not come to him at once, but as he lay there he felt weightless, as if his limbs were like dry ice, their density and solidity vanishing; as if the spaces between the atoms that constituted his physical body were now greater than the distances between the stars. As if his whole being was a vast emptiness.

Four

The conversation that changed everything took place not long after Bobby had been elected as a member of parliament, in the early 1980s. Bobby was in the habit, once or twice a month, of having lunch with his father-in-law in the members' dining room at the House of Commons. Derwent White was not a member of the Cabinet, but was still regarded by those in the know as an *éminence grise* within his party. He had the ear of The Lady, and acted as broker between different factions, cutting deals and trading votes. Bobby noticed that people were careful around Derwent White: he was seen as someone who, despite his lack of any official position, could make or break the career of any new member with aspirations to rise in the political world.

'How's Margaret?' Derwent asked, as he always did when he sat down with Bobby. 'She's fine,' answered Bobby. He poured a glass of claret for each of them. 'She wants us to get away for a few weeks during the summer recess, but we've just redecorated the flat and I'm rather hard up at the moment. I wish the other Margaret hadn't frozen our salaries.'

'The Lady's frightened of what they might say in the *Sun*,' his father-in-law told him. 'It doesn't look good for us all to be awarding ourselves a pay increase when the country is in recession. But there are plenty of ways in which you can make up for it.' Then he told Bobby about the new rules that had been brought in to cover members' expenses: the 'additional costs allowance' worth up to twenty-three thousand pounds a year; the 'incidental expenses' provision worth up to seventeen thousand pounds.

'You just have to know how to use the system,' Derwent White continued. 'It's all perfectly fair and above board. If you know what you're doing, you ought to be able to increase your income by at least ten or fifteen thousand a year. The Fees Office knows the form. They aren't too fussy about receipts and they rarely ask any tricky questions.'

Bobby thought about this for a moment, then said, 'But thanks to your generosity, Margaret and I now have a flat in London with no mortgage or anything like that to worry about, so I don't suppose I can claim for living costs when I'm in town?'

Derwent White tapped the side of his nose with his finger. He was a tall, thin man with an abundance of silver-grey hair who wore charcoal-grey suits of immaculate cut and a regimental tie. His presence was so commanding that he could get away with stagy gestures.

'You have to understand that this new system is really a way of helping MPs to keep up with the cost of living. You have to be creative,' he told Bobby. As soon as he said these words, there was a part of Bobby's brain that lit up with warning signs. He was a lawyer by training, after all, and he knew that what Derwent meant was that there were, in fact, rules. What he was being told was that he could circumvent those rules. He could be creative.

'How do you mean?' Bobby asked, his tone cautious. Derwent White knew his son-in-law liked to follow, rather than lead, so he leaned across the table until Bobby could see the silver hairs curling inside his nostrils.

'See that chap over there?' Derwent White indicated an opposition MP whom Bobby knew by sight. 'He paid off his mortgage last year. I happen to know that because he told somebody who told me. But he's still claiming the mortgage payments on his Additional Costs Allowance. The Fees Office never asks for statements. It just pays the money, regular as clockwork.'

'You mean —' began Bobby, but Derwent White cut him off.

'*I* don't mean anything. I'm simply explaining to you, as an older member, how things work around here.'

When lunch was over, Derwent White went into the City to attend a board meeting of the merchant bank that employed him, and Bobby went away to think things over in a corner of the House of Commons library. An additional ten thousand pounds a year was a very tempting prospect. He had no outside interests, and no income other than what he earned as a member of parliament. He had not, until now, taken advantage of any of the various allowances available, beyond the bare minimum that he could justify through the presentation of a few modest receipts for travel up and down from his constituency. Now he was being told that the expenses system was like the udders of a well-fed cow waiting to be milked.

Bobby told himself there was no harm in doing what his father-in-law had advised him to do. 'You're a fool if you don't,' Derwent White had said after the second or third glass of claret. 'Why leave money on the table?

It's there for you to take, and if you don't, someone else will.'

Bobby now saw, too, another way of boosting his income. He could let the small house they owned in his constituency. All he needed was a room for the few nights a year he spent there. Margaret hated the town whose interests Bobby represented and refused to travel there with him, except once a year for the Conservative Association garden party. 'Ghastly suburban place,' she called it.

Then again, might he also not make more use of the allowances available for staff and secretarial help? Perhaps he should set up a company with Margaret as the sole shareholder – as Derwent White had suggested – and that company could bill him for secretarial services, and he could pass those bills on to the Fees Office. In that way the Fees Office would, in effect, be paying Margaret her dress and housekeeping expenses. Nobody would either know or care about it.

As soon as he had designed in his head a system for claiming money to which he was not entitled, Bobby knew he was doing something that was not right. As he sat in the library thinking it over, he almost decided not to do it. But then Margaret would continue to complain about their lack of holidays abroad, or say that her car needed replacing. It was not that she was spoiled, Bobby would explain to himself, it was just that she was used to a certain standard of living. Derwent White looked after himself well, and he was generous to the rest of his family. It wasn't unreasonable for Margaret to expect that the good things in life should continue to flow towards her, even if they now came from her husband. And all her friends, who included in their number the wives of other

37

MPs, would be having their holidays abroad. No doubt some of their husbands would be using the very same expenses system he was hesitating about using.

Bobby did not make any decision that day, or even that week, but within the month he had submitted his claim for mortgage interest as if nothing had changed. He found that his conscience did not trouble him as much as he had expected, and after a year he had successfully buried the whole business at the back of his mind. Every now and then his brain would send out a bat squeak of conscience, like a signal from a navigation beacon far away, telling him he was off course. It wasn't just about the money, though. Bobby submitted his claims to the Fees Office because that was what most of the people he knew – most of the people he knew whose good opinion he wanted to keep – did, and he didn't want to stand out from the crowd.

His career in parliament flourished, in a modest way. His father-in-law did not interfere, but Bobby was conscious that he had been invited to sit on this or that committee not entirely as a result of his own merits. In the late 1980s Derwent White retired and left the House. Bobby came out from under his shadow and started to gain recognition as a hard-working, dependable backbencher. Nobody would ever ask him to do a job that required exceptional intelligence or the gift of public speaking, but there were many other jobs to be done: boring, tedious jobs sitting on committees, appearances on local radio to explain the Government line on this or that. Bobby did all those jobs willingly. The radio and press reporters liked him because he gave a straight answer, and when he didn't know the answer he said so. The party whips liked him because he never asked tricky questions and would never have dreamed of abstaining when his vote was needed, much less voting against the Government line.

Maybe his enthusiastic use of the expenses system would have mattered less if he hadn't campaigned in the general election in 1992 on honesty in politics. That was when the first whisperings of 'sleaze' began to be levelled against the Government – as they are against any government when it has been in power for too long. The whisperings were not yet as loud as they would become, but Bobby campaigned on the simple slogan: Bobby Wansbeck – Fighting for Honesty in Politics and Your Local Interests.

It was not much of a slogan, but that was Bobby's pitch. He couldn't claim he had achieved a great deal during his time in parliament, but he could say – he felt – that he had been straight-talking and plain-speaking. When he addressed public meetings, he would often begin by saying: 'I'm not one of your high-fliers. I'll never sit around the Cabinet table, or be sent to Brussels, nor do I want those things. My job is to represent *you*, here in this town, and to make sure *your* voice is heard in Westminster. With Bobby Wansbeck, what you see is what you get.'

But what the voters did not see was the share register of Exco22 Ltd, sole shareholder Margaret Wansbeck, bills for secretarial services paid into the company by Bobby Wansbeck, no taxable profits thanks to various invented overheads, and all its revenue ultimately coming from the Fees Office – which derived its money from the taxpayer. Nor did the voters appreciate that every month they were paying for a mortgage that had been paid off nearly ten years ago.

Sometimes Bobby would wake up in the middle of the night and worry about it all. He never suspected for a moment that his affairs would be made public – it was simply a question of his own personal conscience, his lawyer's conscience that had not been entirely extinguished over the years. He would open his eyes and look at the pattern of the streetlights reflected on the ceiling and think: 'I really ought to pack it in. It isn't right.' But then he would remember the outgoings on the tiny villa they had bought outside Saint Tropez in the south of France; he would think about his membership of two fairly expensive golf clubs; he would think about the new Mercedes E200 he had his eye on. Then he would admit to himself that the extra fifteen thousand a year came in handy and would be impossible to replace if he gave it up. What would Margaret say if he suddenly announced that they would have to sell their new holiday home, with its pool and sun terrace and its distant view of the Mediterranean? He was quite sure she wouldn't be pleased.

Her father had died in 1991, not long after the political assassination of Margaret Thatcher in late 1990, as if he, too, had been stabbed in the back. By that time Derwent White was no longer an MP and had felt exiled from his own party. The 'men in grey suits' finished his heroine's career, and the anger and disappointment Derwent White experienced after the event probably contributed to his death at the relatively young age of seventy-three.

At his father-in-law's funeral Bobby wept. Margaret said: 'I've never seen you cry before.' She herself was dry-eyed. 'You shouldn't take on so. Daddy had a good life. He was never short of anything he wanted. How hateful if he had got really old and ended up dying in some home?'

'It's just,' said Bobby, recovering himself and blowing his nose, 'he was like a real father to me. I never knew my own father.'

'Yes, you've often said. He bolted, didn't he?'

'We never quite knew what happened to him. He was a partner in a firm of solicitors and was about to be charged with fraud for dipping his hands into a client account.'

'You've never told me *that* before.'

'No, well, it's not something I'm proud of. Mummy thought he probably couldn't face the shame of it. He just took off when he was found out and nobody's heard from him since. I don't even know if he's still alive.'

'Well, Daddy made most of his money from share tips he got while he was working at the merchant bank. Nobody ever complained about that, although I dare say it isn't so different in principle to what your father did.'

When Derwent White's will was read out, it turned out that there wasn't that much money left. He had been a rich man, but had lived extremely well and denied himself nothing: shooting grouse and pheasants sixty days a year, and belonging to all the clubs Bobby belonged to and more. So there wasn't much of an inheritance: the directorial fees and the proceeds from the insider dealing appeared to have all been spent. Yet again, Bobby decided it would be imprudent to give up his Fees Office top-ups – at least for the moment.

And so it went on. Bobby didn't do anything about it and didn't often think about the matter. It was only that – just occasionally – a voice inside would tell him that his whole career was a monument to effort rather than ability, propped up by a reputation as a simple but honest man. And that monument was built on sand.

But it didn't matter. It really didn't matter. Everyone did it. Nobody minded, or at least nobody cared about what was going on, even if the occasional waspish article about MPs expenses did surface in the press from time to time. Life went on as it had always done. Until one day in May 2009, he came down to breakfast and Margaret showed him the article in the *Daily Telegraph*.

Five

As Bobby came down the staircase the next morning for breakfast, a young woman hurried out of the dining room followed by a child, a boy of about six years old. The woman – although to Bobby she appeared to be not much more than a girl – caught his attention at once. She was striking. Bobby first glimpsed her in profile and saw an aquiline nose, a chiselled mouth, and glossy brown hair swept back from her forehead and tied with a band. Her complexion was an olive brown and she had an elegant, thin figure. She turned her head and said to the boy: 'Don't dawdle. Or we'll be late.' He saw that her eyes were brown with very clear whites. She spoke with the clear elocution of the Home Counties.

As she spoke, she gave the boy a look in which irritation and profound love were mixed in equal measure. But the boy was standing still at the foot of the stairs and gazing up at Bobby. In his stare was a kind of recognition, but it wasn't recognition because it couldn't be recognition. Bobby had never seen the boy or his mother before, and they had never seen him. The boy's mother did not look at Bobby but, realizing her son had stopped, she turned and took him by the hand, pulling him, firmly but not roughly, in the direction of the hotel entrance.

It was only when they had gone that Bobby felt a strange feeling of déjà vu. Surely he had seen them before somewhere? And not just somewhere – he had seen them here, in this very hotel, at the foot of this staircase. Then he corrected himself: it was a trick of his memory. He knew about déjà vu. Most people experience that strange sense of familiarity at least once in their lives, sometimes often. It was a sensation that suggested a person or a landscape – that hedge, those windblown trees – had been seen before, as if the person seeing them for the first time had lived another life, perhaps centuries ago, visited that lane with the hedge and the windblown trees in a previous existence. But Bobby knew that this sensation was an anomaly. The probable cause was the part of the brain where memories are stored disconnecting and then reconnecting a millionth of a second later. It was that briefest of gaps, as the memory rebooted itself, that created the illusion of having seen something before.

Thinking of memory, perhaps reflections of this nature would be an interesting way to open his memoir. After all, if one could define the nature of memory, one could better describe what it is that one was remembering. And what we remember defines who we are. He would have breakfast in a moment; first he must capture these thoughts before they were scattered by the taste of coffee and warm bread and cool butter that were waiting for him in the dining room.

Bobby went back to his room and found that the maid, working at a speed that suggested only a cursory attention to detail, had already made up his bed. However, he could find no fault with her work: the room was immaculate and he could see her trolley with its mops and stacks of

44

clean laundry outside the adjoining room that was separated from his by a locked door.

Bobby sat down at the writing table and opened his notebook. He unscrewed his fountain pen and inscribed the heading he had decided on: *Thirty Years In the Trenches: A Memoir by Robert Wansbeck*. He thought for a few minutes, trying to capture the ideas that had occurred to him as he gazed at the young woman and her son. Then he wrote:

Where does memory of the past stop and experience of the present begin? The answer is that there is no present, because by the time we have experienced that sip of wine, it is already in the past. We remember the taste of the wine, and we sip again to confirm our memory and overlay the first memory with another. There is no present, only a memory of what we call the present. And if there is no present, how can there be such a thing as the future? The future is simply a projection of our memories. We live within our memories. We are trapped by our memories. Only by understanding that, can we ever be freed from them. Each individual remembers only his or her own reality, and that reality can never be truly shared. We live not in one universe, but in a multitude of selfish universes, as far apart from one another as the distant stars . . .

Bobby stopped writing and read the words he had put down. That wasn't quite what he wanted to say. He didn't know where those thoughts had come from. He had intended to start with a few sentences about his early years as a barrister, working on criminal law cases, before

45

he heard the call to go into politics. But he could use this passage somewhere in the book, perhaps in a prologue. If Margaret had been here, he would have read it out to her and she would have appeared to listen and nodded her head. Then, when he had finished reading and was waiting for some word of praise or a critical comment, she would ask: 'What did you just say, dear?'

He would say something, trying not to show his annoyance, and then she would ask another question: 'Disastrous invasion of Turkish beaches, nine letters across, ends in an "I"?' And he would rack his brains for a moment in order to give her the answer to the crossword clue she was busy with, and his train of thought would be lost.

But that was life with Margaret. It had its ups and downs – and its *longueurs* – just as most marriages did; although, in truth, Bobby had no idea what other people's marriages might be like. He could no longer remember his own as clearly as one might expect after thirty-seven years spent sharing his life with someone else. He and Margaret had undoubtedly been happy together. He supposed they must have been happy because, otherwise, why would they have stayed together for so long? But at that moment, he could not remember either unhappiness or happiness. He supposed that, after a while, in the balance scales where these things were measured, the unhappiness had outweighed the happiness – for Margaret at least. Otherwise, why would she have left him?

That was a good question. Why *had* she left him? He could not now remember the particular event, if there had been one. He did remember Margaret coming to see him in hospital and sitting beside his bed while he breathed in and out, the only form of self-expression of which he was capable at the time. The tubes that were connected to him gurgled in harmony and as his chest rose and fell, he had brief moments of consciousness. And whenever he was awake, she was sitting there patiently, waiting in case he should say something, or even just acknowledge her presence with a flicker of his eyes.

At what point had she left him? Was it while he was still in hospital? Or was it after he had returned home, during his convalescence? That would have been uncharacteristic of her. She valued kindness and loyalty in others, so he had always assumed she must value these qualities in herself as well. But he could not remember exactly when she had left. It seemed strange to him that he could not remember and he felt he ought to be more worried about this gap in his memory than he actually was. Memory was treacherous. He knew that much.

In any case, there must have come a moment when, realizing he was on his own and without commitments, he had begun to plan this holiday. He had chosen the hotel without properly consulting Margaret and had made the travel arrangements for a single person, so he supposed she was no longer with him by the time he did that. Still, it was odd that he could not remember either why she had left him, or when.

And now he had missed breakfast. He rose from the writing table, conscious that the sun was higher in the sky and that the morning was passing. He did not want to waste another day doing nothing. Not that it mattered: he could stay here for weeks if he wanted to, even months. But it was against his nature to fritter away time. He changed into his walking clothes – a very lightweight tweed cloth he'd had made up by his tailor into something

47

like a shooting suit – and put on his boots. At Reception he stopped to make some enquiries, but the receptionist was busy in his cubicle, talking on the phone, and he could not manage to get the man's attention. No matter. There was a small display stand on the desk with leaflets detailing local attractions: the zoo in the nearby city where he had arrived by train; the opera house in the same city (unfinished and without a roof as the result of a banking collapse, it was now being marketed as a 'modern ruin'); and then various local attractions. Bobby leafed through these: the vineyards where the local wine was produced; a nearby castle complete with dungeons and a torture chamber; the fishing harbour, about one kilometre beyond the village; and the monastery of Saint Christopher.

Bobby studied the leaflet describing the monastery. It was written in a form of English:

The Monasterium of San Cristoforo may be easily reached on foot by one hour walking from the Hotel. Please be noted that the church-boys [he supposed this meant the monks] are making religious vow of silence and may not be permitted for chats with the Tourist Visitor.

A passable map showed that one simply had to cross the road next to a well, and pick up a path that wound up the side of the mountain. It was as easy as that.

He left the hotel and walked down the drive to the main road. On the other side he could see the lip of a stone well. He walked across – no sign of any traffic in either direction – and paused by the well. There was a bucket and ladle chained to it that could be lowered by turning a handle. Bobby decided he would try the water. He wound the handle until the bucket hit the surface with a splash about twenty feet below, and then jiggled the rope until the weight at the other end told him he had shipped some water into the bucket. He hauled it up and looked closely at the liquid inside. The water looked clean and cold, but when he sipped some from the ladle it tasted bitter and metallic and he spat it out immediately.

He started up the path. Long ago, someone had set paving stones into it. These were now worn and smooth and covered with the white dust that was everywhere, but the going was easy and the gradient gentle at first. On either side of the track was a hedge of myrtle or some similar plant that gave shade and shelter from the wind to the traveller. The hillside above was stony and covered in scrub. If it were not for this path it would be a very difficult scramble, but Bobby saw that he was gaining height with surprising ease and stopped for a moment to admire the view.

Below he could see the roofs of the hotel and its attendant buildings, and the little promontory that it guarded. A yacht was sailing across the bay, cutting a white wake and heading away from the hotel. He wondered if it had called in there to drop someone off or pick someone up. Not far beyond the hotel, he could see the village: a single main street with a few alleys running off it. He could make out the church and, behind it, a building that looked like a warehouse and was newer than the rest. Beyond that a side road ran down to a small harbour and he could see half a dozen fishing boats tied to a jetty, their nets drying in the sun. And past that a landscape of orchards and olive groves and the occasional low, white building. He could see a faint haze in the far distance, and thought it might be the town where he had disembarked from the train.

But the haze was not, in fact, confined to the town. The light dulled for a moment and, looking up, he saw that the sun had gone behind a cloud. The sky, which had been a universal blue when he had set out from the hotel, was now dotted with small clouds and the light was weaker than before. He heard the clinking of bells and spotted a herd of goats coming down the path towards him, led by the bellwether, a glossy-looking animal with brown hair and a curled lip. The goats ignored him as they trooped past on their elegant, small feet. There was no goatherd with them. The animals in this part of the world were an independent lot, he decided.

Bobby walked on steadily as the track slanted this way and that. Above him he could see a cliff and wondered how on earth he would get up it. He thought the monastery must be above it somewhere. He had been walking for at least an hour, and even allowing for the inaccuracy of the leaflet whose directions he was following, he ought to be within sight of the place soon. The light was now much greyer than before, the sun had gone in and the temperature was dropping, but the exertion of his walk kept Bobby quite warm enough.

The track was now lined on either side with boulders rather than shrubs, and it wound its way cunningly up the side of the cliff, underneath overhangs dripping with moisture from the streamers of low cloud or fog that had begun to track across the hillside. Then the paving stones became a stone stairway and Bobby climbed at least a hundred steps before suddenly emerging at the top of the cliff. In front of him was the monastery.

At first, his main feeling was one of disappointment. The cliff he had just climbed was the first in a staircase of cliffs, and a great wall covered in a white limewash abutted one of these and then joined, at the other end, an enormous boulder that had split off from its parent rock epochs ago. In the middle of the wall was a tall wooden gate. It was shut. Beside the gate was a cast-iron bell, suspended from the wall on a bracket, with a chain dangling from it. And that was all. The wall was too high to see what might lie beyond, but it was tantalizing. Bobby imagined courtyards in which the monks sat or walked in pairs. He imagined a chapel; cloisters; refectories and chapterhouses. He imagined a pond full of carp; he imagined a garden full of apricot trees; he imagined a dusty library full of manuscripts bound in vellum. But whatever might be behind the wall would remain a mystery unless he could get through the gate. There was no other way around, even for a rock-climber.

Very well, he would see. He walked up to the gate and pushed it. It did not yield. He felt a sense of frustration that was almost anger. To have come all this way! He then noticed the chain dangling from the bell and pulled it. There was an iron clang and a fluttering noise as a flight of ravens took off from the rocks and pinnacles on either side of the wall, settling back on their perches as the peal of the bell faded. Bobby felt like any traveller might at any such gate: both expectant and wary as to what might appear on the other side. What would he say to a porter or monk who came in answer to the bell? And in what language would they reply, if they spoke at all, for he now remembered that the leaflet at the hotel had said the monks belonged to a silent order?

Indeed, someone was coming. Bobby heard the click of a lock being turned and then, very slowly, the gate opened. It did not open far, just enough to allow the person on the other side to peer through the gap. It was a monk: a tall, thin man with a shaven head dressed in a brown habit. The monk looked straight at Bobby but did not see him, and after a moment Bobby realized why. The monk was blind. His eyes, or what could be seen of them under the drooping lids, were milky-white and without pupils. The monk did not speak, but raised a finger to his lips in the universal appeal for silence. Then the gate shut again and the key turned in the lock.

There was no point in hanging around if that was the sort of welcome on offer. Besides, now that he had stopped moving, the chilly mist was making him feel cold. Bobby had read that these mountain monasteries were famous for their hospitality: that the weary traveller could always rely on them at the very least for a drink of water and, in some places, wine, hot stew and a bed for the night might be offered. Not on this occasion. Bobby retraced his steps and began the awkward descent of the stone staircase over slabs and sills slippery with moisture.

At last he regained the path. The wind was getting up, thinning the low cloud that clung to the side of the mountain. It was just as well, because at first Bobby could barely see five yards in front of his face. Then he began to see a little further and was startled to notice, a hundred yards or so below where he stood now, the black outline of a gaunt figure standing beside the track with its arms outstretched. For a moment he felt almost alarmed. Who could it be, waiting for him down there? There was no doubt, from the attitude of the figure, that

52

it was expecting *someone*. The thought flashed through his mind that it might be Margaret. She had followed him to the hotel, obtained directions from Reception, and was now waiting for him below, prevented by the mist from climbing any further.

If it were Margaret, what would he say to her? Would he be dismissive, or welcoming? The mist was now displaying a strange luminosity as the sun attempted to penetrate it. Drops of dew glittered like diamonds on every rock, and on every branch and leaf. If it were Margaret, he thought, with a rush of love that alarmed him even more, he would take her immediately in his arms and tell her all the things he ought to have told her over all the years they had known each other: the things he had never said, the affection he had never shown.

But then he realized how absurd the idea was. Margaret could not possibly have followed him here. He had told nobody at the hotel where he was going. He doubted she even knew in which country he was staying, let alone that he could be found on this particular path. So, if not Margaret, then who was the dark figure standing on the path below, its arms outstretched hungrily, appearing and disappearing as the wind blew the streamers of fog about the hillside?

Then the sun burned through at last and Bobby was able to see more clearly the outline of a dead olive tree near the track, its branches outstretched like arms.

Six

Bobby remembered the conversation at breakfast in their London flat. Margaret was – unusually for her – already reading his newspaper before he sat down at the breakfast table. He felt a momentary irritation: he liked the newspaper to come to him pristine and uncrumpled. Margaret always managed to make it look as though it had been in a spin dryer after she'd had it in her hands for no more than a few minutes.

'This doesn't sound too good,' she said as Bobby sat down.

'What doesn't sound too good?'

She raised the paper so that he could read the headline: Four Ministers Who Milked the System. Bobby took the paper from her, earning a surprised: 'Oh, really, can't you wait until I've finished?' and scanned the article. It was about the misuse of the allowance and expenses system by some members of parliament. At the bottom it said: 'The *Daily Telegraph* has learned further details of MPs who have misused the expenses system and plans to publish a series of articles over the next few weeks.'

'Haven't they got anything better to write about?' he asked Margaret. She shook her head in irritation, but it was not clear whether she was irked by the scandal-mongering of the newspaper, or by the fact that Bobby had taken the paper away from her before she'd finished reading the article.

As it turned out, the newspapers didn't have anything better to write about: for what could be better than this? Over the next few weeks, more and more details appeared in the *Telegraph* and were then repeated, or enlarged on, in other newspapers. At first, Bobby couldn't see how the story had any relevance to his own personal affairs. He even had a quiet chuckle with friends about the discomfiture of the first politicians to be named: after all, they were all on the Government benches and he was, and had been since 1997, an opposition backbencher.

That was before the phone call from his agent, Charlie Weatherford, a few months after the scandal first broke. The better-known politicians whose expenses were not above reproach had already been named and shamed, but the appetite of the press – and its readers – had not abated. A constant trickle of new allegations continued to surface, as reporters mined the original material for more details.

When Charlie rang, he didn't even say hello, but started the conversation with the remark: 'You're in the papers tomorrow, Bobby.'

'Am I? Why is that?'

Bobby thought that it might have something to do with the Bypass campaign. Or else the Delegated Powers and Regulatory Reform Committee, of which he was a member. But no journalist had contacted him in recent weeks.

'You mean you haven't heard?'

'I haven't heard a thing. What are you talking about?'

'I'm talking about you being named with a dozen others as someone who fiddles his expenses. Is it true?'

Bobby suddenly felt very short of breath.

'Of course not.'

'But they are going to say you claimed mortgage interest on your London flat. Except that they claim you haven't had a mortgage for years. Is *that* true?'

'I would have to check my records.'

'You mean you can't remember whether or not you have a mortgage?'

'Well, no. I'm not aware of my accountant claiming for such payments. As I said, I'd have to check.'

Even to Bobby's ears, this sounded unbelievable. Charlie Weatherford sucked in his breath.

'The newspaper is going to say that the taxpayer has been paying for your non-existent mortgage. It's also going to suggest you have been claiming for services provided by a company which is, in fact, wholly owned by Margaret.'

'I don't see what's so wrong with that.'

'The newspaper,' continued Charlie, 'is going to say you were able to claim mortgage payments on your London flat because your main home is in your constituency. I must admit, I knew you didn't spend much time up here, and I know we never see Margaret, but I didn't know you had rented the whole bloody house out to somebody else.'

Bobby tried to keep his voice from shaking.

'No, hold on, old boy, you've got the wrong end of the stick. I do keep a room for myself there. Mr Singh just pays a bit of rent and looks after the place while I'm away.'

'Don't you see how this looks, Bobby? Don't you *get* it?'

'I'll have to look into it. My accountant may have made an error about the mortgage payments. If there's an error, obviously I will put it right. But the rest of it – don't you think you're making a mountain out of a molehill, Charlie?'

'I'm not the man writing the article, Bobby. I'm ringing to warn you that you could be in a lot of trouble. And I suppose I was expecting to hear you say something that might have put my mind at rest.'

Bobby's feelings of alarm were rising, almost threatening to choke him, but he struggled to keep his tone casual, as if the whole matter was hardly worth talking about.

'I'd better read the article and see what all the fuss is about. I expect they've got it all wrong, as usual.'

'You'd better call me again when you've read it,' said Charlie, and hung up. Bobby could tell Charlie was very unsettled, but that was his agent's job, he supposed: to worry about things. He tried to push the conversation to the back of his mind but, all the same, he was conscious of the acid bubbling in his stomach, and a dull sense that bad things were to follow. This became an ache in his side, as if the worry had nested itself within his body. The phone call he had just received was the moment he thought would never come, the thing he had told himself again and again not to worry about. Then, in the afternoon, while he was in the members' lobby, his mobile rang.

'Bobby?' an unfamiliar voice asked. Bobby looked at the screen. It said: Unknown Number.

'Who is this?'

'Mike Williamson,' said the voice, 'from the *Gazette*.'

The *Gazette* was the local paper in Bobby's constituency.

'Would you care to comment on Exco22 Limited?' asked the voice. 'The main shareholder is your wife, isn't that right?'

'What is this about?' asked Bobby.

'You've been paying Exco22 Limited fifteen thousand pounds a year and claiming the money as secretarial and management services, right?'

'I have claimed nothing except what I am entitled to,' said Bobby. He sounded pompous even to himself.

'Yeah, yeah. And you also claimed mortgage interest of another ten thousand pounds a year on a flat in London. Our investigation at the Land Registry shows there hasn't been a mortgage on this property since 1982.'

'I cannot comment. Everything I have done has been above board. Ask anyone in my constituency. Everyone knows I have worked tirelessly on my constituents' behalf.'

'We will ask, Bobby, don't you worry. Would you like to make any other comment before we publish this story tomorrow?'

Bobby couldn't think of a single word to say. He experienced a moment of blind panic and hit the disconnect button. The phone rang again, several times, but he ignored it. Surely nobody would take these muck-raking journalists seriously?

When the articles appeared in the national and local papers the following morning, Bobby read them with the same sick apprehension he used to feel when reading his school reports. These were a lot worse. There was no 'must try harder'; indeed, no prospect of redemption was offered at all.

In the days that followed, it became clear that not only were people taking the stories in the papers seriously: they actually wanted them to be true. It was a kind of revenge on the political classes, somebody told Bobby – somebody not mentioned in any lists of MPs and who could therefore afford to be philosophical about it all.

Bobby stopped sleeping. He couldn't believe that someone had ferreted around in his private affairs and discovered that he had no mortgage. He couldn't believe that his arrangements with Exco22 Ltd were being discussed in public, let alone called into question. He tossed and turned at night and his sheets were damp with perspiration in the morning. Margaret told him to move into the spare bedroom, and he did. The problem was there was nobody he could really talk to about all this. Margaret wasn't much help.

'I expect it will blow over, dear,' was all she could think of to say. His father-in-law, to whom he used to take his problems, was long dead and his own agent seemed very unhelpful when Bobby rang back to ask his advice.

'What should I say, Charlie?' asked Bobby. 'People keep on ringing me and asking me for comments. What should I tell them?'

'Don't ask me, mate,' said Charlie. 'You presumably had a reason for claiming for a non-existent mortgage and paying your wife all this money on expenses. What was it?'

'Oh, for God's sake, say something helpful!'

There was a pause. Then Charlie said, 'All I can think of is this: tell them what you told me. Tell them it was an accounting error. Tell them that since the House of Commons Fees Office approved the payments, you assumed everything was in order. Shift the blame onto your accountant, or the Fees Office, if you can. And, above all, tell them that if an error is proved to have occurred, you will pay back anything you weren't entitled to.'

'But that could be hundreds of thousands of pounds over the last twenty-odd years. I couldn't possibly pay all that back.'

'Then sell the bloody flat.'

There was a long silence. Bobby's hand had become so damp that the phone almost slipped from it.

'Well thanks, Charlie. That's a great help. Thanks very much.'

'Look, Bobby,' said Charlie.

'What?'

'This isn't any good, you know. Down here in the constituency, people are hopping mad with you. They think you've been ripping them off. They feel it's money taken from their pockets and put into yours.'

'Then defend me, Charlie. That's your job.'

'No, that isn't my job. My job is to keep this constituency voting Conservative. With you as MP, that might be next to impossible come the next general election. And that can't be many months away.'

Bobby and Charlie didn't speak very much over the next few weeks. Bobby received a letter from the Fees Office telling him that it believed he had wrongly claimed £29,755.93p in the last two accounting years. He was invited to provide copies of the building-society statements to show the balance of his mortgage that remained unpaid. He was also invited to provide details of Exco22 Ltd and the services it provided, and who its shareholders were. The Fees Office would be glad to receive his proposals for repayment of any money incorrectly paid to him.

This was possibly the nicest letter Bobby received during those weeks. With every morning's post there came more letters mostly, but by no means always, from his constituents.

Dear Mr Wansbeck,

I cannot tell you how disappointed my wife and I were to learn of your fraudulent expense claims. I am sorry to put it so strongly but I can think of no other

60

word. We voted for you because you said you were an ordinary citizen representing the views of other ordinary people like yourself. And all the while you were feathering your own nest.

Dear Bobby,

You might remember me from our schooldays together. I strayed from the path of righteousness ten years ago, when I was convicted for aggravated burglary. But in prison the Lord came to me, and the Lord set my feet on the right path. Bobby, I am praying for you. Listen to the Good Lord in the watches of the night. Yea, he will come. Yea, he will speak to you . . .

You Fuckin Toff I Hope You Rot in Hell. (This last scribbled on a scrap of paper torn from an exercise book.)

And with every letter the ache in his side grew. Bobby began to lose weight. He went to see the doctor, who told him it was stress: what did he expect?

'I'm not right,' Bobby told Margaret.

'I expect it's a bug. A lot of people have been feeling under the weather recently. Which reminds me, Simon and Emma have cancelled. We were supposed to be having dinner with them tomorrow night but Emma says she isn't feeling one hundred per cent so, you see, you're not the only one.'

'I don't want to go out to dinner anyway.'

'You don't suppose . . . it couldn't be . . . they're not cancelling us because of this silly expenses nonsense?'

'Quite possibly,' said Bobby. 'In fact, that seems to me a much more likely explanation.' He scratched his side.

'Don't do that,' Margaret told him. 'You're scratching yourself like a monkey. It's not very attractive, dear.'

'I can't help it. I'm itchy.'

The itching had been getting worse for a while now. That was bad enough, but then a few days later he started vomiting. He never knew when it was going to happen. Once it struck on the Tube, when he was jammed in the middle of a very crowded carriage on the Piccadilly Line. The good news was that he had a Sainsbury's bag with him, so he vomited into that – to the disgust of his fellow passengers – rather than on the floor of the train. The bad news was that there were four lamb chops and some asparagus spears in the bag that had been intended for supper. After that, supper didn't seem like such a good idea anyway.

He went to see his GP again. His GP told him once more that he was suffering from stress, and his tone was unsympathetic. Bobby imagined he'd been reading the papers, just like everyone else. Every day brought fresh revelations about spurious or doubtful expenses claims from MPs on all sides of the House. Bobby had the scant comfort of knowing he was by no means the only MP in trouble. Unsympathetic or not, the doctor did take some blood from Bobby for analysis and arranged for Bobby to have a CT scan.

Charlie Weatherford rang to tell him he'd better come down to the constituency and face the music at a meeting of the local Conservative Association.

The doctor rang to say the blood test showed elevated levels of immunoglobulin.

Bobby went and had his CT scan. He was now beginning to worry that there really might be something wrong with him, but he never seemed to have any time to think about it. He was called in for an interview with the chief whip. This was so like going before the headmaster after some awful offence at school – smoking behind the cricket pavilion – that it was almost laughable.

'It's not looking good, Bobby,' said the chief whip. 'Our dear leader is keen for the party to be squeaky clean by the time the present incumbent of number ten calls an election.'

'I quite understand,' said Bobby. 'There have been some awful stories getting into the papers. But I hope you agree that, in my own case, we are simply talking about an accounting error. Regrettable but, as you know, I keep myself very busy and sometimes things are overlooked.'

The chief whip looked at him for about a minute before he replied and Bobby began to feel uncomfortable; also nauseous. He wondered if he might have to dash out of the chief whip's office in a moment before he redecorated it in a manner not likely to uplift his approval rating.

'You see your problem in that light, do you?' asked the chief whip. 'Because that's not how it looks to us. Are you all right, Bobby? You've gone a bit green.'

'I'm not feeling great,' said Bobby. 'Must have been something I ate.'

The interview didn't continue much longer. The chief whip said he rather feared Bobby would be invited to stand down before the next election, if he didn't want the embarrassment of being disbarred from standing again as the candidate for his party. Bobby said he'd listen to what his constituents had to say before reaching any decisions. The interview ended with just enough time for Bobby to race to the nearest available men's room and throw up.

When Bobby arrived home that evening, after a long afternoon session in the House that went on into the evening, he told Margaret that he was going to have to visit the constituency.

'I have to go down there tomorrow, darling. Charlie Weatherford wants me to show my face.'

Margaret looked put out.

'But you know we are going to the opera tomorrow night. You can't possibly cancel. Think how much the tickets cost. And *La Bohème* is one of my favourites. So sad.'

The visit to the opera would have to wait, Bobby told Margaret, and she would have to give his ticket to one of her friends.

The following afternoon, Bobby took the train from King's Cross. He had arranged to be met at the station by Charlie Weatherford. He was by now feeling so uncertain of even Charlie's loyalty that he felt a certain relief when he saw his slight figure standing next to the ticket barrier, clad in his usual scruffy wax jacket, pullover and corduroy trousers. Charlie's greeting was minimal, however, and there was no handshake. They climbed into his old Isuzu Trooper and drove in silence in the direction of the town hall. Bobby felt obliged to say something in order to get Charlie to speak.

'Are we expecting a big turnout, Charlie?' he asked.

'The usual people. The ones who gave you their time and knocked on doors and handed out leaflets for you at the last election: maybe forty or fifty of them. You've lost weight.'

'I'm on a diet,' said Bobby.

They arrived at the town hall, a red-brick building that dated back to the beginning of the last century. On the way in, a young man stuck a digital recorder in front of Bobby's face and said, 'Mike Williamson, the *Gazette*. Are you going to be deselected tonight, Mr Wansbeck? Will you be offering your resignation?'

'This is a private meeting,' said Charlie, pushing past the reporter. 'Mr Wansbeck has no comment to make until he's spoken with his constituents.'

They entered the debating chamber, which had a platform with an oak lectern in the middle, facing a small auditorium with tiered seats. Less than half the seats were occupied. On the platform stood the local party chairman, the secretary and four chairs. Bobby shook hands with everyone, then strode with as much self-possession as he could muster up to the lectern and waited for Charlie to open the proceedings. It was usual at these meetings for Charlie to make some reference to all the good work Bobby had been doing in Westminster on their behalf: a sort of warm-up act. This time he simply stood up and said, 'Bobby Wansbeck is here to make a brief statement and will then take any questions you may have.'

He sat down again. Bobby's mobile rang at that moment and he had to pull it from his pocket before he could turn it off. He'd forgotten all about it. As he pushed the buttons, he saw that it was his doctor calling. Oh God, what now, he thought to himself. Then he did his best to pull himself together and made a short speech.

He reminded everyone that he had served his constituency for thirty years during which time, he said, he had worked tirelessly on their behalf. He was proud to have represented them for so long and to have enjoyed their confidence in so many elections and he would like to remind them, if he might, of some of the good things that had resulted from his representation. There was the new pedestrian crossing, right outside the town hall. There wasn't a Tesco: his battle against the supermarket giant had protected the jobs of many local high-street traders. And there would soon – although no precise date could be agreed until after the next election – be the new bypass, that would transform the quality of life of everyone who lived in the town centre, some of whom he knew were here tonight.

He wouldn't speak, he said, of his endless work on the many parliamentary select committees he had sat on over the years. It might bore them to death, he said, forcing himself to laugh, but he could assure them that bad as most of the legislation introduced by the present govern-ment might be, many new bills coming before the house had been rescued from total disaster by the work of such committees. Nobody else in the hall laughed. His audience just sat there, stony-faced and silent.

Bobby added a few words about the importance of retaining the experience of MPs such as himself if the party took power at the next general election. Then he said: 'I have been unfortunate enough to have had my name linked to what is called the "expenses scandal". I just want to say a few words about that. This is trial by the media, without judge or jury, or any chance of a defence. As far as I am concerned, I have done nothing wrong. I freely admit there is a possibility, which I am looking into, that I may have been in error in claiming certain expenses from the Fees Office, but we are talking about accounting matters, not my integrity. If the Fees Office can show I have been paid any sum of money in

66

error then I will, to the best of my ability, repay whatever is owed. That is all I want to say at present.'

Then he left the lectern and sat down on one of the chairs. Charlie Weatherford stood up and asked if there were any questions. There was a long silence. Bobby fought the urge to scratch his side, which felt as if it was burning. Then a tall, thin man in a battered corduroy jacket stood up. Bobby recognized him as one of the leaflet-distributors, but had forgotten his name. Charlie whispered in Bobby's ear: 'Bill Atkins.'

'I work as a teacher,' said Bill Atkins. 'I earn thirty-two thousand pounds a year. That's what the country values my services at. Fair enough. You're an MP. I believe you earn sixty-five thousand pounds a year, give or take. Then I'm told that the taxpayer subsidizes your pension to the tune of seventeen thousand pounds a year. Is that more or less right, Mr Wansbeck?'

'Yes,' said Bobby. He knew what was coming.

'So why do you feel it necessary to claim expenses of as much as another thirty thousand pounds a year, Mr Wansbeck? That's a total package of over a hundred thousand pounds a year: more than three times what I am paid. Accounting error or not, do you think that's right, Mr Wansbeck?'

There was murmuring in the hall. Somebody at the back shouted, 'Resign!'

Charlie Weatherford stood up and said, 'Let's keep this civilized if we can.'

'How much money have you and your wife ripped off the system in the last few years, Bobby?' shouted a woman sitting next to Bill Atkins. Another man stood up: a large, heavy-set man with a ruddy complexion, dressed in a pinstriped suit. Bobby recognized him as a generous donor to local party funds. It was Peter Morgan, the managing director of a local chemical company that was part of a big multinational.

'Mr Wansbeck, if I claimed thirty thousand pounds of expenses from my company that I wasn't entitled to, and then tried to say it was an accounting error, do you know what would happen to me? I would lose my job on the spot. I would be sacked for gross misconduct and then I would probably be prosecuted for theft. Do you think you should be treated any differently and, if so, why?'

After that remark, the evening went downhill and what had begun as a meeting became more like a low-intensity riot. After twenty more minutes of this, Charlie managed to bring proceedings to a close and shepherded Bobby out of the hall. Outside there were more reporters and a man holding a placard that read: Bent Politicians Should Rot In Hell.

By this time Bobby was feeling rather numb, but he did wonder whether the man with the placard was one of his recent correspondents. He got into the car with Charlie, his shirt sticking to his back with perspiration and his head aching. As Charlie drove him back to the station, Bobby switched on his phone and listened to his voicemail. There was a message from his doctor, telling him that there was a possibility he might have pancreatic cancer.

'We need to carry out some more tests,' he said. 'There's something showing up on the scan that might be a problem and we should certainly investigate it further. Don't be alarmed unnecessarily: it may turn out to be nothing at all.'

Bobby didn't know what that meant. With luck it would turn out to be nothing serious. But recently his luck hadn't been too good.

Seven

Bobby sat at the writing table in his room, remembering. He opened the black notebook on his desk and unscrewed his fountain pen and wrote on the blank and creamy title page: *Thirty Years' Service and Five Minutes' Dismissal: A Life Discarded*. Underneath he wrote: *By Bobby Wansbeck, MP*. He wasn't going to shelter behind some pseudonym; the whole point was that he had nothing to be ashamed of and nothing to hide. He thought for a moment then wrote:

> I can look back with some satisfaction on thirty years of considerable political achievement. We backbenchers may not change the world, but in this book I hope to show how it is the small changes in our lives that endure: not the wars we start as prime ministers, or the taxes we raise as chancellors, but the new hospital that is opened in our constituencies, or the new bypass that is built; the things that affect the ordinary, everyday lives of the people around us. These are the building blocks of real change, not the spin and psycho-dramas that fill the newspapers from day to day . . .

Bobby stopped writing for a moment and reflected on what he had written. What *had* his achievements been? It might be helpful to have a list of them beside him. And that, in turn, might help with his chapter plan. He looked around and found a small notepad by the telephone which he brought back to the desk, then started to write down a list of what he had done, or caused to be done, as an MP.

In fact, he decided, he needed two lists. The first would detail changes within his own constituency, the second changes to legislation he had contributed to by means of sitting on various committees. Under the first heading he wrote: *the new bypass,* then he paused. That had been a huge battle. For most of his time as an MP he had campaigned for money to be set aside from the roads programme to build a bypass around the main town in his constituency, whose high street was clogged from dawn to dusk by enormous container trucks from the nearby port. Time and time again, the shadow transport minister had told him: 'It's not as if you represent a marginal constituency. Spending money in your patch isn't going to make the slightest difference. We'll keep the seat anyway. You haven't a hope.' But, in the end, he had won. The bypass had finally been included in the white paper entitled: 'Consultations on proposals to amend the criteria defining strategic national corridors'. It might not be built in his lifetime, but one day there would be a new bypass and – if there were any justice in the world – it would be named after him.

Time was passing and Bobby realized that if he spent the whole morning sitting writing his memoirs, he would miss breakfast and that would be a bad way to start the day. He closed the notebook and went downstairs. Halfway down the stairs he heard the dining-room door open and, with a curious feeling of déjà vu, saw a woman – not much more than a girl – come out, followed by a small boy. It was an odd sensation, rather unsettling. He felt as if he ought to know the girl and the small boy, as if they were somehow familiar, familiar in ways that bound them closely to him. And yet he knew he had never seen them before in his life. The girl, who was obviously the boy's mother, turned to the child and said: 'Don't dawdle. Or we'll be late.' Bobby was reminded of the white rabbit in *Alice in Wonderland*. He wouldn't have been surprised if she had taken out a pocket watch and examined it. But she did not. Instead, she took hold of the boy's hand – he had stopped at the foot of the stairs and appeared to be gazing intently at Bobby, or at something or someone behind Bobby – and pulled him along behind her through the open front door of the hotel. The boy's gaze had been so fixed, so *knowing*, that Bobby turned to look behind him to see if there was someone else on the stairs. There was nobody. He must have been the one the boy was looking at. But why had he stopped to look at Bobby? What was it about him that the boy found so odd? And what was it he found so odd about the boy and his mother? Why this persistent feeling that they had met somewhere before?

Bobby shook his head as he came down the last few steps. It was, he told himself, only a case of déjà vu. That sort of thing happened sometimes. But the sensation was so strong within him, as if he were standing on the edge of one world looking into another, that he decided he would catch up with the woman and the boy and find some reason to have a word with them. If he struck up a conversation with them, it might occur to him when or where he had seen them before. And if he hadn't seen them before, then he would know it was simply déjà vu.

It occurred to him that the woman had spoken in English and that of itself gave him a reason to speak to her. It would be surprising if there were many other English families here – it wasn't a well-known destination. He could say something like, 'I couldn't help overhearing you just now. I thought I was the only person in England who knew about this hotel.' And she would reply in that familiar cut-glass voice, 'Oh, we read about it in some magazine – how did you hear about it?' And then he would reply, 'I've always known about this place.' And then he realized that while he was standing here having this imaginary conversation in his head, the people he wanted to have it with were getting further and further away.

He hurried through the front door of the hotel. It was like stepping into a furnace. The day was, if possible, even hotter than the day before and the heat hit him like a blow to the face. For a moment he thought about turning back into the relative cool of the hotel lobby – but no, he was determined to speak to the young mother and her child. Where were they, though? He walked down the drive and looked along the road that led to the village. They were nowhere in sight, yet they certainly hadn't been gone that long; it was at least ten minutes' walk to the village. If they had been picked up by a car, he would expect to have heard the noise of its engine and for the dust stirred up by its passage to be hanging in the air. But the only noise he could hear was the endless chirping of crickets on the hillside, a sound that must have been there all the time but had been filtered out as he concentrated on trying to find the two strangers. Apart from that, the silence was absolute. There was not a breath of wind and the hillside above him baked in the heat. He could see a track snaking up the mountain – that must be the way to the monastery

72

that he wanted to visit; he would explore that tomorrow if the weather cooled down a little – but it was empty of any figures. The heat bore down on him and the endless *scree scree* of the crickets was getting inside his head.

He looked the other way and noticed that a path ran around the side of the hotel and back towards the seashore. It would be cooler beside the sea and he thought that this was probably where the woman and the boy had gone. He followed the path which ran down a grassy slope and then around the corner of the hotel with a blank wall to the left and a laurel hedge to the right. Emerging from this tunnel-like section the path then continued below the sun terrace, eventually meeting up with the other path that led through the hotel garden, before meandering along the edge of the rocks and sea pools of the foreshore. Bobby walked on, hearing the sound of people above him on the sun terrace who were hidden by the terrace wall. The path dipped lower and lower until it was just above what he imagined must be the high-tide mark in this almost tideless sea. The hotel garden was behind him now and the ground to his left was much like the rest of the hillside, covered in white boulders and bushy shrubs. On his right were rocks covered in seaweed and a few pools, in between which were beds of fine gravel that looked almost like sand. Then, a few feet beyond, the gentle murmur of the waves, lapping against the rocks, hissing and sucking gently as they ran in between and over them.

Bobby peered ahead and was almost sure he could see the boy and his mother turning a corner, disappearing behind an outcrop of boulders. He should step on it if he wanted to catch them up. The path ran so close to the edge of the sea that it was quite slippery, and there were pools of water here and there, so that even though he quickened his pace he was unable to go fast enough. When he came to the outcrop of boulders, he thought he heard a sweet, childish voice cry out: 'Mummy, look at this shell!' But if he was near enough to hear the boy, he was still not near enough to see him. Beyond the boulders, he could see that the promontory narrowed, ending in a point a few hundred yards ahead. There was nobody in sight. He could see the splash of waves against rocks and feel the freshness of the wind against his cheeks. He realized that he had come out from the lee of the promontory and there was less shelter from the wind; or else the wind was increasing in strength.

As he approached the point, the rocks to his left grew lower and flattened out as if, wearied by the constant battering of the sea, they had decided to lie down to protect themselves. They were streaked with weed and great grooves had been cut by the action of the waves. It was clear that the sea often washed over these last few yards of the land. Suddenly Bobby felt exposed and vulnerable. Looking back, he saw that it was further than he thought to the shelter of the rocks around which the path had brought him; as if to emphasize that fact, a wave suddenly smacked the rocks ahead of him, rising several feet into the air and sending a shower of fine spray that was carried over Bobby on the wind.

Nevertheless, he followed the path onwards and found that it petered out in a little gravel beach right at the end of the headland. There were no footmarks on the fine gravel – nothing to indicate that the boy and his mother had come this far. But they must have done. He saw them. He as good as saw them. He heard them, or at least he was sure he had heard the boy.

But if they had walked this far they would have had to pass him on their return because there was no other way back to the hotel. Bobby clambered over some boulders to get a better view of the other side of the peninsula and his heart sank. For the first few yards the going was the same as on the leeward side, except that there was no path. But then the headland tilted slightly and he saw that on the windward side the rocks slanted down steeply to the sea. There was no hint of a beach, just a steepening rocky slope that became almost a cliff. It was difficult to imagine anyone, let alone a small boy, scrambling over those rocks. What was more, the sea on this side of the headland was distinctly – and increasingly – choppy. He could hear the slap of the waves hitting the rocks; he could see fountains of spray rising up, then falling back on themselves.

He couldn't work out what had happened to the mother and boy. As he stood there, he remembered the words of Sherlock Holmes: 'When you have eliminated the impossible, then the alternative that remains, however improbable, must be the truth.'

It was impossible that the mother and her son should have returned back along the coastal path without coming past him. It was impossible for a woman in high-heeled shoes, or her young son, to have scrambled across those jagged rocks so quickly as to be already out of sight. It was improbable but – and here another wave smacked against the rocks a few feet away sending a wash of spray into the air – not impossible, that they should have attempted to return by that route and either become stuck on a ledge out of sight or, no more improbable, they had been carried out to sea by a wave.

Bobby realized he must go back at once to the hotel for help. He wanted to run, but the path's twists and turns and ups and downs made that almost impossible, and a stiff breeze had begun to blow from the land so that no matter how hard he tried to hurry, the force of it was like the palm of a giant hand placed against his chest. He seemed to be making no progress at all, and all this while the young woman and her son might be in the greatest danger, might even be drowning. He felt a sense of panic. He had come away for peace and quiet and somehow he had become involved, through no fault of his own, in what might turn out to be a tragedy. He imagined the boy and his mother floating face down in the waves, the girl's hair streaming out around her, like Ophelia amongst the lilies.

He lay between the cool, clean sheets of his bed. Night had fallen and the events of the day seemed distant and remote. He had been dreaming, and his heart was racing as the memory of the dream faded from his conscious mind: something to do with drowning, but who or what he could not remember. The wind rattled the window frames and buffeted the headland on which the hotel sat. A spatter of rain struck the glass panes as he gazed, unblinking, out of the window, watching clouds stream across the starlit sky, causing the stars to quiver and go out. Now the night was pitch-black, so dark that it was easy to believe there had never been any moon and there were no such things as stars.

Eight

'I wonder if they will give me a position as a parliamentary undersecretary,' mused Bobby aloud as he sat in the bath. Margaret was at her dressing table in the little room she used for this purpose next to the bathroom. It wasn't much larger than a shoebox, she often complained, but in Chelsea even shoeboxes have their value.

'You've been complaining to me that they might be going to ask you to give up your seat. You've been in such a panic about it all. Quite unnecessary,' replied Margaret. Bobby's comment had been addressed to the bathroom ceiling, but Margaret had overheard it.

'Yes, but that was before half of the party got caught up in the scandal,' said Bobby. 'People have been claiming for cleaning their moats and duck ponds. Even our dear leader has had his wrist slapped over some gardening expenses. If they ask every MP who has had a letter from the Fees Office to leave, then they won't be able to run the House of Commons any more. There won't be anybody left.'

He laughed harshly and then winced as pain flared in his side.

'Are you ever going to get out of that bath?' asked Margaret. 'The taxi will be here in twenty minutes.'

They were going to a champagne reception on the terrace

of the House of Lords. These were heady days. An election was looming. Political scandals filled the newspapers. Party activists were fundraising as fast as they could. Nobody quite knew who was in and who was out in their own party, or which, if any, party might form the next government. Tonight's occasion was a fundraiser to which leading businessmen from around the country had been invited. Whether or not the powers that be had intended to ask Bobby, he had been invited anyway. Perhaps his disgrace had been overlooked, or perhaps it was the fact that so many had been drawn into the net of the 'expenses scandal' that it had been quite hard to find enough MPs prepared to undergo a couple of hours of excruciating boredom, shaking the hands of potential donors.

Bobby climbed out of the bath, towelled himself dry and began to dress.

'I don't see why they wouldn't give me a promotion. It sounds to me as if the party will be desperately short of men with any experience after the election. I honestly don't see how they could manage without us.'

Bobby had his socks and his shirt on now and began to knot his tie in front of the bathroom mirror.

'What did the doctor say this afternoon?' asked Margaret from next door. Bobby had been slow to return the doctor's calls. He had convinced himself for a while that he had enough bad news to deal with without any more worries. Weeks passed before he finally submitted himself for further tests. More weeks had passed while he awaited the results of the investigations.

'Oh, nothing. That is, not exactly nothing but nothing that can't wait. If I start to tell you about all that I'll never be ready in time.'

*

The reception was attended by two hundred well-off businessmen and their wives, together with a scattering of backbenchers. A few big beasts stalked through the crowd trying to look like the secretaries of state they hoped they would soon become.

At first the party was like any other: a lot of noise, waiters circulating busily with glasses of something intended to pass as champagne; lots of shoulder-slapping and arm-grasping and bone-crushing handshakes amongst the men; women eyeing up each others' diamond rings, necklaces and brooches, trying to decide which were paste and which were real.

Bobby had long ago developed a technique for such occasions. He would clasp someone's hand with a firm grip and say something like, 'I'm so glad to have met you at last. We really are very grateful for everything you have done for the party. You know, it's impossible to talk properly at these functions. It would be so good if you would let me give you lunch at the House some day, when you have an hour or two to spare. Will you do that? Just call my office – forgive me, but there's someone over there I really have to speak to. So nice to have met you.' And so on, and so on. Margaret sometimes accompanied him on these sorties, but she preferred to stand with a little group of other politician's wives, amongst whom she was acknowledged as a minor queen, on account of who her father was.

At first this party seemed much like any other. Bobby shook hands and issued thanks and invitations without really taking in who he was talking to. And then a hand that he had reached out to grasp was withdrawn and he heard a familiar voice say, 'What the bloody hell are *you* doing here?'

It was Peter Morgan, the businessman from Bobby's constituency who had questioned him about his expenses a few weeks ago. Bobby had been on autopilot and simply hadn't noticed who he was speaking to. So many faces to remember, and memory was so treacherous to him.

'Oh, Peter,' he said weakly. 'So good of you to come tonight.'

Peter Morgan was a big man with the physique of a front-row forward. He looked down at Bobby and said, 'I didn't come here to waste my time talking to you, that's for certain. I thought you'd been dropped. It's a bloody disgrace . . .'

The sound of his voice, rising in volume with each word, attracted the attention of a passing big beast. The big beast interposed himself between Bobby and Peter Morgan and said, 'I'm so sorry. I don't know how his name got on the list. Someone hasn't updated our records. He shouldn't have been asked – I completely understand how you feel.' He drew Peter Morgan away so that Bobby could no longer hear what was being said. It had all happened so quickly that Bobby was still standing there on his own a moment later, his hand half outstretched and a smile frozen on his face, when someone took his elbow. Behind every big beast there is usually a jackal or two and this was one of them. He pulled Bobby gently but firmly towards the other side of the terrace then said softly into his ear, as if offering – or demanding – a sexual favour: 'Bobby, I think you'd better disappear, don't you?'

'And why should I do that?' asked Bobby, but his indignation was mostly faked and it was obvious in his voice.

'Because you're not wanted. Because some fucking secretary forgot to remove your name from the invitation list. Come on, Bobby, you know you're out. You're dead, you just haven't realized it yet. Find Margaret and take her home. Just get away from here before you do any more damage.'

There wasn't any point in arguing. Bobby knew it would be better to leave while he still had some dignity, rather than endure being cut dead by guests and colleagues alike as word spread. He shook off the jackal's paw and went and found Margaret, who was in the middle of an animated conversation with a friend.

'We're going home,' he told her, interrupting without any apology or explanation. Margaret started to protest, but Bobby pulled her away and said quietly, 'Either we leave together now, or we'll be chucked out. Which would you prefer?'

As they walked towards the exit, Margaret pale and furious, another couple overtook them. Bobby did not recognize either of them and they did not appear to have recognized Bobby.

'What we do for Queen and country,' said the man, laughing. 'What a dreary evening. God, I can't wait to get away from here, can you?'

'I quite agree,' said Bobby.

In the taxi, Margaret sat beside him looking furious and refusing to respond to anything Bobby said. He gave up trying to talk and waited for the explosion he knew would come the moment they were inside the flat.

'Parliamentary undersecretary,' she said bitterly as they came through the front door. 'It's quite clear they want to have nothing more to do with you. What a fool you were to accept the invitation. I've never been so humiliated in my entire life.'

Bobby thought to himself that he had had his fair share of humiliation too, but he also knew that argument would only prolong the row. So he simply said, 'I was sent an invitation. I presumed that meant that they'd decided my accounting errors weren't so very special after all, and they wanted me back on board. It turns out I was wrong.'

'Get me a whisky. A large one.'

Bobby went to the bookcase, found the decanter and two crystal glasses and poured each of them a stiff whisky. They sat in silence sipping their drinks. Bobby could see that Margaret was winding herself up for another angry remark, so he pre-empted her.

'As we're having one of those evenings, I might as well get it over with. I saw the doctor this afternoon. He says I've got cancer.'

'You've got *what*?'

Bobby repeated the announcement, then added, 'It's pancreatic cancer. They're going to operate. I don't know when, but soon.'

'Why didn't you *tell* me?'

'I just did. There really wasn't a chance to tell you before.'

'But just out of the blue, like that . . .'

'You know I haven't been feeling well.'

'Men never feel well whenever there's a problem. I thought it was just your nerves.'

Bobby couldn't think of anything to say to that. There was a long silence.

'They're not going to give you chemotherapy?' asked Margaret after a while. She drained the last of her whisky.

'Nobody's mentioned that so far.'

'Good, because Sheila Mackenzie had chemo and all her hair fell out. You may not have much hair, but some is better than none. I think baldness can be so unattractive. It wouldn't suit you.'

Nothing more was said on the matter, but later that night when they were in bed together, Bobby felt an arm snake around him and a low voice said, 'You'd better not leave me. You'd better not fucking *die*.'

Bobby was shocked.

'Of course I won't die. You'll see. I'm a tough old bird.'

The illness was an inconvenience at first. Then it became more than that. Bobby was referred to a surgeon, a Mr Banerji, who was struggling to find a gap in his busy schedule to fit in Bobby's operation. Bobby didn't feel himself at all these days. He stopped attending the House. There seemed to be no point in going there just to be insulted and, anyway, the House would soon rise and absent itself in preparation for a general election. He did have another meeting in the flat with a smooth young man with well-oiled hair and an immaculate charcoal-grey suit who came from the chief whip's office, bringing with him the paperwork for Bobby's resignation. The man also produced a draft of a short press release stating that Bobby was resigning his seat on the grounds of ill health.

'It gives us time to parachute in your successor,' he explained, 'although the poor man will have his work cut out. There's only five weeks to go.'

'If I agree to this, will you guarantee I get my resettlement grant?' asked Bobby, his pen poised above the papers he had been asked to sign. A resettlement grant is the equivalent for MPs of a redundancy payment and is worth around sixty-five thousand pounds, so it was not to be surrendered lightly. The smooth young man raised an eyebrow.

'Nobody's cutting you any deals, Mr Wansbeck. You can either sign now or be disbarred from standing again as a Conservative candidate. Anyway, it's not up to the whip's office to make decisions of that sort.'

Bobby signed the papers anyway. He felt too ill to argue. These days he spent most of his time lying on the sofa and chewing the occasional painkiller. He daydreamed about telephone calls to come:

Bobby – it's all been a dreadful mistake. Number ten was horrified to find you might be leaving us. We're all in the same boat with this expenses nonsense. There's no way we are going to let your thirty years' of experience slip through our fingers. Our new prime minister is talking about a meeting – very private, off the record – can you come?

Mr Wansbeck – Mr Banerji here. I've been looking at your scan again. The radiographer has made a mistake. It's not cancer. It's a simple gallstone. I'm so sorry you've been put through all this worry.

But the phone never rang. Even the press had given up calling. The general election campaign had begun and there were new dramas each night on the television. Bobby couldn't bear to watch any of it, and he couldn't bear to read the papers. He lay on the sofa, much to Margaret's annoyance, who was used to having the flat to herself during the daytime, and he gazed at the ceiling and he asked himself a question: Was there ever any choice? I am the son of a man who stole money from his clients, and I've become a man who will be remembered as one of those who stole money from the voters. Did I ever have any choice? Wasn't it in my DNA? Could I really have helped myself?

He knew that for the last thirty years he had presented himself as an honest man when he had been nothing of the sort. He knew that, if he told nobody else the truth, he had at least to be honest with himself, as far as he was able. He knew that there *had* been a choice. And he thought that his life could have turned out quite differently, if he had chosen differently. He knew that guilt had been corroding him for years, and that underneath his smooth outer surface there was very little of the original Bobby Wansbeck left. Because that is what guilt does: you end up telling so many lies that you no longer remember who you really are. You can no longer believe your own memories.

So Bobby lay on the sofa and waited for the call that would summon him to the hospital.

Nine

Bobby sat at the writing table. Weak sunshine filled the room, followed by shadows as clouds raced across the sky. It looked too windy to go outside for a walk, and Bobby had decided that today he would start to make some notes for his great project: the memoirs detailing his political life that would re-establish his reputation as a politician of the highest integrity, a man of sound judgement and experience.

Last night he had lain awake remembering the way in which his career had come to an end. But memory is treacherous, he thought. Had that awful meeting in the town hall really happened, or was it one of the morphine dreams that happened afterwards, when he was ill? He unscrewed the fountain pen that lay on the desk and shook it, then pulled the black notebook towards him and opened it at the first page. The blank space seemed inviting. He set down the words *Backbencher: The Life of a Political Journeyman.* As a title, that was modest enough. He wrote:

Over the years I have often been asked: what is the most important characteristic to look for in a politician? There are plenty of different answers one could give: tenacity, a way with words, strong political convictions. But I have always answered that question very simply with a single word: 'integrity'. For if a politician is not true to himself, then he is nothing – true to himself, and true to the people who voted for him.

Some members – I may say this is more the case nowadays than it was when I first came to the House in 1979 – feel they are a failure if they are not appointed a junior minister, or at the very least a private secretary, within the first year or so after their election. I have never taken that view. I will never be remembered as someone who introduced a bill for reforming the voting system, or for protecting the rights of this or that minority. I doubt I will be remembered at all. But if I am, I hope it is by a motorist in my constituency who will say, as he speeds along the new bypass that I fought for, for so many years, 'Thank God old Bobby Wansbeck dug his heels in about our local road network.'

Bobby paused and laid down his pen. True to himself, and true to the people who voted for him. He had always been that. He thought of himself as a good foot soldier, loyal to his party, loyal – but not unquestioningly loyal – to the whip. A backroom boy, a hard worker who shunned the limelight and got things done. He thought of himself as an old-fashioned Tory: Queen, Country, Party.

And he had always been true, apart from that one little slip. If he examined his actions closely, he would allow that the way he had claimed his expenses could be made to look wrong. But it wasn't wrong. Nearly everybody did it, especially when a previous prime minister had frozen MPs' salaries. It had been well known in the lobbies and bars that what the right hand taketh away, the left hand giveth. It was the system. You claimed your expenses up to the limit and beyond, if you could make a case for it. That was the entitlement. It wasn't his fault Margaret's father had decided to pay off their mortgage. Why should he claim less than another man, just because of an accident of fate such as that?

Bobby had been cast on the scrapheap for doing no more than what he believed was common practice. It was a technicality. He had been abandoned by his party and by his constituents for this minor breach of some mysterious rulebook which nobody ever read. He had been sacrificed to make others look good: to make others look strong and decisive. Thirty years of long evenings spent in a stuffy chamber, listening to other members droning on. Thirty years of insufferable sherry parties in his constituency. Thirty years of being at the centre of events, one of the country's legislators, shaping and directing the world in which ordinary people lived. And now he had been cast out without a thought for all those hours and weeks and months and years of service.

He put down his pen. He wasn't in the mood for writing. Whenever he started to write, the memories came flooding back. It seemed as if the wounds still had not healed, even now. But he was determined that he should not waste his precious solitude in this hotel. It was an opportunity to take stock of his life. He just needed to achieve some detachment, a sense of perspective.

Every time he wrote something down about his life, the words seemed mean and small, as if his whole career had been invisible and pointless. And yet he believed he had been, nearly, a great man. Not everyone can be Winston

Churchill. Bobby had never been front of the house, but that didn't mean his life was unimportant. Only – why had it been important? What had ever truly given it meaning?

He stood up. Outside the wind had dropped and the sun was more brilliant than ever, heat shimmering in the air. The paving stones on the terrace looked as if they might cook you if you walked on them. He went downstairs and crossed the entrance hall to the door of the dining room. Through the frosted-glass panes he could hear people talking – in fact, it sounded like an argument between a man and a woman – but he could not see who was inside. At any rate, they should still be serving breakfast and he was hungry. He turned the handle of the dining-room door but the door wouldn't budge. It must be locked. He rattled it for a moment. The sound must have been audible in the other room, but nobody came.

In disgust, Bobby turned on his heel and walked to Reception. There was nobody about. On the counter was a bell, so he rang it. He waited, then rang it again. Leaning over the counter he could just make out the figure of a woman bent over a ledger in the back office. The glass-panelled door was closed and she obviously hadn't heard him.

'Excuse me,' said Bobby loudly. The woman still didn't hear him. There was no sign of the concierge. Come to think of it, he hadn't actually seen a concierge although, in a hotel such as this, there must be one.

'EXCUSE ME!' shouted Bobby, his frustration getting the better of him. The woman in the back office paused, licked her forefinger and turned another page in the ledger. She must be deaf. Was everybody in this country either blind or deaf? It was beginning to seem that way. For a moment Bobby thought of making a real scene: going behind the counter, storming into the office and shaking the woman by the shoulders. But what was the point? If the poor woman couldn't hear him bellowing like that she probably *was* deaf.

He made a conscious effort to relax. This was supposed to be a holiday – an extended physical and mental convalescence – and losing his temper was not going to help him. He turned and went upstairs, back to his room. The bed was already made up, so at least that department of the hotel was functioning efficiently. He sat on the edge of the mattress, picked up the phone and dialled nine for Reception. There was no dialling tone. He listened intently, but the phone didn't ring. It didn't even appear to be connected at the other end – except, wait a minute, there was a crackling sound. Maybe there was a loose connection somewhere in the network. He could hear distant voices singing some kind of marching song. The voices were too faint for him to make out the words or even the tune, but he was certain it wasn't English. Maybe the phone was somehow picking up a radio signal. At any rate, it didn't work. He stood up, at a loss. Why had he come back to his room? He couldn't remember: something to do with breakfast.

He went downstairs again and halfway down he saw a young woman coming out of the dining room. She was attractive: dark-haired and olive-skinned, probably Italian from the look of her. She had an elegant, thin figure. In tow was a small boy of about six. As she turned to say something to the boy, Bobby saw that there were tears running down her face. When she spoke it was in English: 'Don't dawdle. Or we'll be late.' She spoke without a tremor, but the tears were real. Then she and her son – he supposed the boy was her son – went out of the front door.

90

Bobby continued on his way to the foot of the stairs and was about to turn left towards the dining room when he paused. The woman was upset about something, perhaps more than upset. Ought he not to go and see what was the matter? She might be quite alone here; she might have a problem she couldn't deal with. He felt he should follow her and ask if he could be of use to her in any way. Besides, there was something familiar about her and the boy: their faces haunted him, irritating the surface of his memory.

He walked to the front door and looked down the drive, but there was no sign of them. He walked down the drive to the point where it joined the dusty white road that led to the village and there was still no sign of them. He hadn't heard, couldn't see, any sign of a car or a bus. Perhaps he might catch them later, somewhere in the hotel. It was too hot to stand outside for very long: hot, and also muggy. The air felt stifling and the intense light was giving him a headache. As he turned to go back inside he saw, on the horizon, a bank of towering purple and black clouds. The sky around them was an ominous yellow – it looked as if a storm was building out to sea.

Bobby went back inside the hotel. As he crossed the hall, he saw a newspaper that had been left lying on an armchair. He hadn't noticed it before and would not have taken any notice of it now, except that he saw it was an English paper. He didn't know you could have English newspapers delivered here. He would order one to be delivered to him if that were the case. On the other hand, this might have been brought here by one of the guests: the girl he had seen earlier, for example. The newspaper was, on closer inspection, the *Daily Mirror* but it looked different, somehow: it must be an overseas edition. The headline said, Council Rents May Now Go Up With Pay.

Bobby picked it up and examined the front page more carefully. The date on the masthead was 30 June 1954. It must be one of those facsimile editions that people bought as presents for one another, to commemorate a birth date, and so on. He scanned the paper briefly: not a very interesting day in history, as far as he could see. Then he put it down and went upstairs.

As he entered the room, he heard a rap at the window and went across to see what had made the sound. A large, fat raindrop had struck the glass and was rolling down it. It was followed by another, then another. After a moment the patter of rain ceased. The sky above the hotel was still cloudless, but the air had thickened even in the last few minutes. The sunlight was turning dull and hazy and the cloudbank he had seen earlier was approaching, and now stretched from one end of the horizon to the other. As Bobby watched, a flicker of lightning jumped between the clouds. The sea was glassy calm. He could feel the electricity in the air.

The tension seemed to communicate itself to him. He felt as if he could no longer concentrate on any one thing, as if the power of rational thought was passing from him. He walked across to the writing table to see if he could make some progress with his memoirs. He sat down and opened the black notebook. The pages were blank. He was quite convinced he had written down something earlier in the day: in fact, only an hour or two ago. But he must have imagined it.

He wanted to write his memoirs, but memory was slipping from him. He could feel it draining away. He didn't know what was happening to him. He was stuck in this hotel. God knows why he had come here. He could never find any staff. He couldn't remember when he had last eaten – he was sure he hadn't managed to have breakfast today. There had been a problem with the dining-room door; that was why he hadn't eaten. What kind of hotel locked its guests out from the dining room? And where *were* the other guests? Apart from the woman and her son whom he had seen this morning, there didn't seem to be anybody else about. He had heard other people; he thought he had seen them too, but he hadn't spoken to anybody at all. He hadn't intended to have an active social life while he was staying here, but he hadn't intended to become a hermit either.

Bobby opened the window and leaned out, but there was nobody on the sun terrace below. The flurry of rain must have sent them all indoors: but where? He left his room again and walked along the corridor. On impulse he tried a couple of the other bedroom doors. They were all locked. He went downstairs to the reception counter, but there was nobody there and the woman he had seen earlier in the back office was no longer at work. He looked for the English newspaper he had seen earlier, but somebody had tidied it away. He went to the dining room but the dining-room door was locked. He went through the other public rooms: a smoking room, a lounge facing the sea full of shabby armchairs. There was nobody sitting in any of the armchairs. He went down a corridor towards the staff quarters but there was nobody about. He found the swing doors that led into the kitchen, but the kitchen was empty too. Not only were there no people but there were no signs of recent activity – just empty marble and steel counters, and a huge and ancient-looking range of ovens that were cold to the touch.

He went back to Reception, went behind the counter and tried to open the door of the back office. He had some idea in his mind of finding the hotel register to see who else was staying. There must be other people here somewhere. But the back office was closed. On the wall was a clock and below the clock was a calendar consisting of a cylinder with three windows: the kind where you turned a handle and different days and months and years appeared. He pressed his face against the glass panes of the door and saw that the date displayed was 30 June 1954.

Bobby lay on his bed and watched the sky darken. The flickers of lightning were more frequent now and he could see them with his eyes closed as well as open. A wind had sprung up again ahead of the advancing storm and he could sense it wrapping itself around the hotel, buffeting it, testing its strength. Rain, or perhaps spray blown in from the sea, began to spatter against the window. There was a rumble of thunder and the sky turned as black as night.

Ten

He remembered the Intensive Care Unit.

He lay there in a morphine dream, surrounded by tubes and wires connected to various bottles and machines that were designed either to keep him alive, or else to inform any interested parties if he were no longer alive. He couldn't tell what was real and what wasn't. He awoke from the operation feeling very sore until some fluid or other kicked in and the soreness went away. He slept. He woke again and it was dark. The clock on the wall of the ICU said half past midnight. Maybe that was real, and maybe it wasn't. The voices sounded real enough. He thought he could hear two male nurses talking in hushed voices in the next cubicle.

'We've instructions from MI5 to turn off his life support at six a.m.,' said the first voice. Bobby thought that the voice belonged to a red-haired porter who had wheeled him into the ward from the operating theatre. He wasn't sure he had ever heard the man speak on that short journey but, if he had, Bobby felt sure his voice would have sounded like this one.

The second voice was much deeper. It asked: 'Why six a.m.?'

'We want to announce his death on the eight o'clock news on Radio Four.'

Bobby struggled to open his eyes, and to clear away the cobwebs that seemed to float in front of them. He didn't know if he was awake or not.

'Why does he have to die?' asked the deep voice.

'Just orders, isn't it? Personally, I think it's because he betrayed his party. They won't stand for it, you know.'

'Well, I dare say he won't be much missed. But I've never killed a man before.'

'It's just a question of pulling out some tubes. You get used to it.'

Bobby faded into unconsciousness and awoke again a little later, or else he dreamed that he was awake. It was still dark and now the male nurse with the deep voice was talking to a female nurse who had joined him in the next cubicle. The red-haired porter must have gone.

'I've always loved you, but I've never dared tell you before.'

'But why tonight?' asked the woman's voice.

'Because in an hour's time I'm going to do something that might mean I will be put away for a very long time.'

'Put away?'

'Sent to prison.'

'But why, Roger?' asked the female voice in a low wail. 'Just when you've told me you love me?'

'It's for the good of the country. That's all I can say.'

Bobby fell asleep again and when he awoke, it was broad daylight. He deduced the assassination plot had failed, or else it had all been a drug-induced dream. Later on – hours or days later, he could not tell – he was wheeled from the ICU and onto a ward.

He slept.

*

96

When he awoke, Bobby was feeling a little more rational. He had been admitted, he'd had an operation and he had survived it. His throat felt more parched than he could imagine a throat could ever be and his lips were cracked. He groped around to find the button he knew must be on his bed somewhere, in order to ring a nurse and ask for some water. But there was a tube inserted into the back of his hand, connected to a bottle on a stand beside the bed, that prevented him from reaching the button. He lay like this for some time until a nurse turned up at his bedside.

'Now how are we today, young man?'

His mouth was so dry he could hardly speak.

'. . . thirsty. . .'

'Nil by mouth for the next two days, petal.'

The nurse checked some charts at the foot of his bed, then went away. He lay there. Now he knew what it might feel like to be abandoned in the Sahara. He descended into a vivid dream in which he was crawling on his hands and knees across gravel plains while the sun burned overhead. A feeling of coolness inside his mouth awoke him. Someone was dabbing his lips and inside his cheeks with a chilled sponge on a stick. He opened his eyes and an angel disguised as a middle-aged nurse – a different nurse – was ministering to him. A few drops of moisture from the swab trickled into the sides of his mouth and its cool taste was wonderful.

The next time he awoke, Margaret was sitting in the chair beside his bed. She was talking to him, and was in the middle of some story, the beginning of which he had missed.

'So then I said to Susan that she shouldn't have made an opening bid of two no trumps.'

Bobby couldn't understand what she was talking about, and said so, rather indistinctly.

'I was just chatting away to you about my bridge evening last night, and waiting for you to wake up. How are you feeling, dear?'

'Never better,' replied Bobby.

'Now, Bobby, don't be sarcastic. I'm doing my best to entertain you.'

He made an effort and they chatted about people and places Bobby could hardly remember. It was like looking at the world, and Margaret within it, down the wrong end of a telescope. Everything seemed very distant. He fell asleep again and when he awoke, Margaret was gone. She had left copies of *Country Life* and *Golf International* on the chair, but Bobby couldn't reach them and didn't feel like reading anyway. A man in a white coat swam into view.

'Hello. I'm Mr Banerji. I'm your surgeon.'

'Oh,' said Bobby. Then he felt he ought to say something more so he said, 'Thank you very much.' Mr Banerji made a brushing motion with his hands as if saving a man's life was not worth commenting on. Then he said, 'It is not very good news.'

'No?'

'We couldn't complete the procedure. The tumour was inoperable. It was much bigger than it appeared on the scans and it has metastasized. There are secondary growths here – and here – and here.'

Each time Mr Banerji said 'here', he prodded Bobby very gently in a different place.

'So, what does that mean, exactly?'

'You are quite ill. We can try chemotherapy, but not at

98

present. You are too weak from the operation. We will have to see how the disease progresses.'

Bobby fell asleep again. The information meant nothing to him. He was quite incapable of thinking about the future. Dealing with the present was almost beyond him. He dozed and slept and dozed. Margaret came back, so a whole day and night must have passed.

'So exciting. That nice young man David Cameron is trying to form a government with the Lib Dems. Can we switch on the television in here?'

Margaret pointed to a screen on the other side of the bed that was attached to a metal arm so it could be swung in front of the patient. Bobby hadn't noticed it before. Margaret examined the contraption.

'Oh, it needs a credit card. I don't think I've remembered to bring mine with me.'

'Never mind. What has happened?'

'They had the election while you were having your operation.'

Bobby remembered that he had gone into hospital on the eve of the general election. Margaret now gave him a slightly disconnected narrative of the momentous events that seemed to be going on in the committee rooms and chambers with which he had once been so familiar. He found he didn't care very much any more.

'What happened to my seat? Did the new chap get in?'

'Yes, but with a *much* smaller majority than yours, dear.'

It had not occurred to Margaret that the reduced majority might be a reflection on Bobby, not the new man who had replaced him at the eleventh hour. He winced.

'Are you all right?'

'Just a twinge. I'm fine.'

After a while Margaret left again. An orderly arrived with the tea trolley and handed Bobby a cup of hot, sweet tea. One or two tubes had been removed from him, which meant he could sit up. The tea tasted better than anything he had ever drunk in his life. A few minutes later, he was sick, but he was still grateful for that first taste of hot liquid.

He began to feel a little more human. When Margaret came to see him the following day, he was quite ready to take part in the conversation with a bit more animation and interest. But it was Margaret who now seemed a little out of sorts. He asked her a few questions about what she had been doing, a subject she usually never tired of, but this time she did not respond.

'What's the matter?' he asked her. 'You seem to be a little bit under the weather.'

'I've just been talking to that nice Indian doctor.'

'Mr Banerji?'

'Yes.'

Margaret delved into her handbag and took out a tissue and blew her nose. She said, 'He told me you haven't got very long to live.'

This was news to Bobby. He hadn't really taken on board what the surgeon had said to him a couple of days before, except that the operation hadn't worked and they were going to try something else. He took Margaret's hand and patted it.

'Don't worry,' he told her. 'Doctors are like weather forecasters. They may be right in the long run, but they usually get the timing wrong. I'm sure I'll keep going for a long time yet.'

Margaret made an effort to smile. He could see how worried she was and made an effort to cheer her up.

'We'll go on holiday when I get out,' he told her. 'Somewhere warm.'

Margaret loved holidays, and lots of them. She brightened a little and said, 'We could go down to the villa for a week or two, if it hasn't been sold.'

Bobby had put their little villa outside Saint Tropez on the market as soon as he realized he might have to stand down as MP.

'No, that would be too sad. I don't want to go there again until we absolutely have to, to clear out our things. No, I had another thought . . .'

Into his mind came the image of an old-fashioned hotel he had been to long, long ago. It stood on the neck of a small headland that jutted out half a mile or so into the Mediterranean. The memory had a curious resonance: a mixture of happiness and great sadness, but he could not remember why.

'It's a lovely place,' he told Margaret. 'I just can't quite remember the name of the hotel, but I'll look it up as soon as I get out of here. I know exactly where it is. I'm not sure if there's an airport nearby these days, but it can't be too much of a struggle to get there. It's the most heavenly place, quite unspoiled. There are no nightclubs, no restaurants with tourist menus, no crowds. The food is absolutely wonderful. The place used to have a Michelin star. No, not a Michelin star exactly, but anyway, it was the best food I ever tasted. And the staff are so friendly, and so discreet. You hardly know anyone is there, but everything is immaculate. You want for nothing. Staying there is more like being at a well-run country house party than a hotel. And the countryside around it is beautiful. The views are to die for.'

Bobby realized he'd been talking for rather a long time, so he stopped. Margaret was looking at him with a strange expression on her face.

She said, 'I don't think I've heard you show so much enthusiasm for anything for absolutely years. Of course we'll go there, darling, if that's what you want.'

For an instant she looked as though she might weep. Bobby put a hand up to her cheek.

'It will be wonderful,' he told her. 'You'll see.'

'When were you last there?' asked Margaret. 'You've never mentioned this place to me before.'

'It was a long time ago. A very long time ago,' Bobby told her. 'But it's still there, I'm quite sure. And it won't have changed. It's not the sort of place that would ever be developed.'

'Of course it won't, darling,' said Margaret. 'I do love you. Try to get some rest. You're overexerting yourself.'

'It won't have changed a bit,' Bobby reassured her. He felt very drowsy and lay back on the pillows. 'It's the most heavenly spot. The views are to die for.'

He slept.

When he next awakened, it was the middle of the night and the overhead lights had been switched off. There was nobody else in his ward at present and the only illumination came from the corridor outside. He wondered why he had woken up. He was hot. His head felt too large and at the same time light, as if it might float away like a balloon down the corridor. Then he heard voices and knew that it was the night nurses with their trolley, coming to take his blood pressure and temperature, and to feed him more pills. For reasons Bobby could not guess, this procedure always took

102

place at two in the morning. The night nurses on this shift were both male. They came into Bobby's ward cheerfully, talking to each other as if they were trying to compete with the roar of a football crowd or a passing train.

'Now then, Bobby,' said the first nurse. 'Time for your gin and tonic.'

He handed Bobby a paper cup in which a tablet of soluble Paracetamol was fizzing in some cold water. Bobby drank it, and then they put the blood-pressure cuff on his arm and stuck a thermometer in his mouth. They did not seem satisfied and his temperature was checked again.

'How are you feeling, old son?' asked the second nurse.

'Sleepy,' said Bobby. 'A bit hot.'

He dozed off and when he awoke again, a doctor was bending over him, shaking him gently by the shoulder.

'Whassamatter?' asked Bobby.

'I just need to take some blood,' said the doctor. 'Your temperature is a bit on the high side.'

Bobby submitted to this procedure, and felt a faint prick as the needle went in.

'Have they decided who is to be prime minister?' he asked the doctor. 'I'm a little out of date. Is Gordon Brown still in number ten?'

The doctor seemed surprised.

'Don't worry about all that,' he replied. 'Try to get some rest.'

'But I'm a member of parliament,' said Bobby energetically. 'I have a right to know. I should have been consulted. I need to get dressed.'

'You're not very well at the moment, Mr Wansbeck. I think you might have picked up an infection. Now try to sleep.'

103

The doctor disappeared and Bobby fell asleep again. He dreamed about the hotel he had told Margaret about. The sun shone down out of a cloudless blue sky and he and Margaret sat on the sun terrace. Or perhaps it wasn't Margaret who was with him. The sea was the same blue as the sky so that it was hard to tell where the water ended and the sky began. He could feel the heat and the light beating down on his closed eyelids. He opened his eyes and found that he was lying on a hard bench with a bright light overhead. Then a feeling of warmth and wetness went right through him and, turning his head, he saw that a new tube had been taped to his right arm, with a needle going into his skin just inside of the elbow.

'We're going to do a scan,' someone whispered. An automated voice told him to breathe in, machinery hummed and clicked, and he was conscious of sliding backwards into a tunnel. He fell asleep again and when he awoke, he was back on the ward. Another doctor, a different one, was shaking him gently by the shoulder. He realized that, while he had slept, they had treacherously attached more tubes and wires to him. A machine was bleeping somewhere nearby.

'How are you feeling, Mr Wansbeck?'

'The truth is,' Bobby replied, 'I don't know how I am feeling. I want to get away from here. I want to go on holiday at the hotel. If I could go away on holiday, I am quite sure I would get better a lot faster than I will staying here, being prodded and poked and fed pills and getting infections. A few weeks in the sun is what I need.'

'Mr Wansbeck? Can you hear me?'

Bobby realized that he hadn't spoken these words aloud. He made a great effort to speak, but he felt so hot, and so tired, and so unlike himself, that he found it difficult to organize his thoughts.

He said, 'It was an accounting error. I have every intention of paying the money back.'

'Mr Wansbeck?' the doctor asked again. Then he heard somebody else say, 'His blood pressure is dropping.'

But Bobby couldn't be bothered to answer. Enough was enough. He was on a journey, on a train, then bumping along somewhere in a taxi – or was it on a gurney – and he knew he was nearly there again, after all these years. The sunlight was strong and warm. Checking in was a mere formality. He went up the stairs to his room, and it had not changed a bit. He walked across the room to the window.

The view was just as he imagined it would be, just as he remembered it.

Eleven

It was dark.

He was awake and it was not yet daybreak. He had the feeling that dawn was still a long time away. Outside, the night sky was starless and moonless. Rain pattered against the windows. From time to time, a gust of wind shook the hotel, but each gust was weaker than the last. The wind was dropping.

He did not know what had awakened him, or if he had ever been asleep. He must have been asleep because he remembered dreaming, although he could not remember what he had been dreaming about. Confused images pursued each other through his mind: he was being wheeled on a bed along a corridor, staring up at bright lights overhead; he was on a train, he was on a journey. And then he had arrived at the hotel.

There was something he had to do, but he couldn't remember what it was at first. For a moment he felt something almost like terror. His mind was as blank as a newborn baby's. He swung his legs over the side of the bed and sat there for a while, trying to gather his thoughts. He realized he had gone to sleep wearing his clothes. At least he had remembered to take off his shoes. He put the shoes on now, bending down to tie up the laces. He saw his tie lying on the bed and put that on too, his hands knotting the tie by memory, something he had done so many thousands of times. He saw that his suit jacket was hanging on the back of the chair beside the writing table. The writing table! He had to write something before he left.

Confusion roared around his head suddenly. What was it that he had to write? For a moment he could not remember: memory, was that not it? Was he not intending to write an essay on memory? Or even his memoirs? He had a vision of himself writing a book in which he justified his life, a book in which everything turned out for the best after all. He stood up and went to the writing desk and put on his jacket. He had to gather his wits. He knew that time was against him, but he did not know why. He felt in the pockets of his jacket and found his wallet. He took it out and counted the money. Just over one hundred pounds, and about the same again in local currency. He kept back what he would need for the taxi to the city, and for the price of a room. He wouldn't need the rest. He put the notes on the desk, and then, worrying that the chambermaid might find them and take them downstairs – or even keep them – he opened the drawers of the writing table, searching for paper and an envelope. There was a leather folder in the drawer. He took out the folder, extracted an envelope and put the money inside, then sealed it. Then he took a sheet of writing paper and began to write.

He found it very hard to say what he wanted. This was because, he supposed, there really was nothing he *could* say. He had lived with lies for so long that telling the truth, even recognizing what the truth was, had become very difficult for him. For so long he had sustained this duality: on the outside, someone whom people could trust; on the inside, something else. He had achieved not exactly eminence in his profession, but a certain standing. He was conscious that people respected him; that he was someone they could turn to for help. But then again he was also conscious that he had betrayed that trust, and had had to smile and go about his business and stand up straight, when all the time the only thing he wanted to do was curl up like a shrivelled leaf and hide himself away.

Well, the hiding part was over. The knowledge of what he had done was out in the open now and would soon become a public scandal. He checked his watch. It was half past one in the morning. The rain had stopped and the only sound he could hear was the *husssh-husssh* of the waves breaking gently on the headland below.

It took him a while to write the letter, and he checked his watch more than once. At last it was finished, and he sealed it in another envelope and put it next to the first. Then he wrote his wife's name on each of them. He stood up. It was time.

The instinct for survival – for life – was still strong in him. He had willed it into submission, but it kept flickering up again, like a candle that could not be blown out. He stood at the window and looked out, but the sky was still unfathomably black. He had thought, in a moment of fantasy, that he might have climbed the hill to the monastery and asked for sanctuary there. But common sense prevailed. They would not have him, and even if they took him in, someone was bound to come looking for him.

There was nowhere else to go, and nothing else he could do, except follow the route he had mapped out for himself. When he had set out from England, he already knew that he was within days of being found out, and of his partners being informed by the auditor what had been going on. But he'd made himself believe that there was still a chance that the whole thing would remain hidden, and that, in due course, he would return home and life would carry on as normal. But, of course, it wouldn't. The letter had come and the game was up. He patted his pockets to check that he had everything he needed. Wallet? Yes. He checked his other inside pocket looking for his passport and pulled out a small brown booklet. On the front it said *Ministry of Food 1953–1954*.

There was a serial number, and below that he had written his name and address. His ration book: why on earth had he brought that along? He opened it and saw that there were stamps entitling him to one banana per week. He smiled wryly. He wouldn't be needing any more bananas. He had not realized he had brought this booklet with him. He placed it next to the two envelopes. He would leave it behind for his wife and their son.

Where was his passport? He would need to have that with him. Ah yes, he had put it in the other drawer of the writing table, the one that could be locked. He found the key and unlocked the drawer. Inside was his passport and an object wrapped in cloth. He took the bundle out and carefully unwrapped it, revealing his Webley Mark VI Service revolver, which he had managed to hold onto after he had been demobbed. When Andrew warned him that several of his client accounts were being checked, he had decided to take the revolver with him. So old-fashioned, he had thought at the time – the revolver and the bottle of whisky were a cliché straight out of an Edwardian melodrama. He had almost put the revolver back in the box under the stairs where it had lain hidden all those years. But he hadn't. And now it didn't strike him as a cliché any more. He stuck the revolver inside the waistband of his trousers. It wasn't very comfortable, but he wouldn't have to put up with the discomfort for long.

It was time to go. He went to the door that connected his room to the bedroom next to his and listened, but there was no sound at all. Its occupants were still fast asleep. All he had to do now was go downstairs without waking anybody and walk up the road to the village where the owner of the pastry shop had agreed to drive him to the railway station in the nearby town. And then he would cover his tracks as best he could, and disappear, as far as the world was concerned. And then . . .

. . . and then all he had to do was find the courage to go downstairs and begin this final journey.

Twelve

The boy sat at breakfast with his mother. She was reading a letter. The holiday had been going perfectly well as far as the boy was concerned, until the letters started arriving. There had been another one at breakfast yesterday which his father had opened. The boy had been sitting just where he was sitting now, in his special seat that the waiters always kept for him, and he had been eating a delicious warm bread roll. When he had happened to look up for a moment, he had seen his father's face turn from a healthy tan to a kind of grey, so that he thought that he couldn't be looking at his own father, but at someone else who had mysteriously taken his place. His mother had been pouring hot milk into her coffee and hadn't noticed anything. Then she looked up.

'What on earth is the matter, darling?' she'd asked. His father had folded the letter and put it in the inside pocket of his jacket.

'Nothing,' he'd said. But of course it wasn't 'nothing'. A letter is always something, not nothing. Even the boy knew that. You didn't get letters about nothing. Your face didn't go a funny colour for no reason.

'Well, what was in your letter? Do tell. I can't imagine who would write to us here. I didn't know anyone had our address.'

111

'I left it with the office in case of an emergency,' his father had said.

'So what's the emergency?' his mother had asked.

But his father had simply shaken his head and said 'Nothing' again and the boy knew that it was a lie. So did his mother.

Then the boy had been told to go outside to the sun terrace and he had complained that he hadn't finished his breakfast, but he went anyway and finished his bread roll sitting on the steps that led down from the terrace to the sea. He had returned a few moments later to look through the dining-room door and see if he could go back inside (and have another bread roll and more jam), but his parents had gone.

He knew they must be having an argument and had felt sad, because this was their first ever holiday abroad and now it was being spoiled. Daddy had been in a funny mood for days, ever since before they went away, and when the boy had told Mummy that he didn't like Daddy any more, she had said, 'He's just tired, darling. He works too hard.'

Then Mummy had come outside to find him and told him that Daddy had gone for a walk to the village. She had looked very pale, as though Daddy's greyness was catching. And Daddy had been away for nearly the whole day and when he came back in time for tea, he had hardly spoken. He had picked up the boy and hugged him quite hard, so that it hurt.

Now it was morning again, and he and Mummy were eating breakfast alone. When he asked her where Daddy was, she just shook her head. The boy watched her when he thought she wasn't looking. Her eyes were glistening.

'Come on, stop staring and eat your breakfast,' his mother told him sharply.

He had always thought his mother was the most beautiful person in the world, with her pale skin that was not white, but a creamy colour, and her thick, brown hair that fell down to her shoulders. He had to admit, though, that she didn't look beautiful today. Her face still had that strained look it had acquired at breakfast yesterday and she was paler than ever. Then he realized that her eyes were not just glistening but that she was crying. Real tears trickled down her cheeks. He had never seen a grown-up cry before. He didn't know they did that.

His mother dabbed her face with the white napkin and said, 'If you don't want any more breakfast, then it's time to go. We've got to go home.'

'But why?'

'Because we have to.'

'But why do we have to?'

'Just for once,' his mother said, 'don't ask any more questions, please.'

'Where's Daddy?'

'He's had to go somewhere, but he will be coming home later.'

'Why is he coming home later?'

Then his mother stood up and said, 'Go outside and play for a bit. Stay on the terrace. Don't go anywhere near the sea. Promise me?'

'What are you going to do?'

'Pack our clothes.'

The boy saw that he really mustn't ask any more questions, so he went and sat on the steps that led down to the sea and watched the waves coming in and going out.

113

They made a sound like someone chuckling at a joke: a secret joke. The sea was glassy smooth and the clouds in the sky were like white sheep in a blue field, except that these sheep were getting thinner and thinner until they disappeared. The day was getting hotter and brighter all the time. The boy thought that this was the nicest place he had ever been. There was any amount of good things to eat, and the people were friendly even if they spoke in a funny way, and the weather was warm. He loved being here, and he didn't understand why they had to leave when he had been told they were going to be here for ages and ages.

His mother found him sitting there an hour later.

'Oh, my goodness, you're getting sunburn,' she said. 'I must put some Nivea cream on that. I hadn't realized it was getting so hot outside.' She held out her hand and Bobby took it. They walked across the terrace and into the dining room. His mother said, 'There's a taxi coming for us.'

'Why can't we stay here?' asked Bobby.

'Because we can't.'

Bobby started to complain, and then he stopped himself. Another tear rolled down his mother's cheek and he realized, without quite being able to put it into words, that something momentous and terrible had just happened and it would change his life for ever. He didn't know how he knew this, or why he was so certain, but he knew it was so.

He was thinking about all this and trying to understand his own thoughts when they went out of the dining room and crossed through the entrance hall at the foot of the staircase. Just then Bobby happened to look up and saw an old man standing halfway down the stairs.

114

There was something terribly sad about this old man, and also something very wrong. He was standing there, staring at Bobby as if his life depended on it, as if he were trying to remember something but couldn't, as if he wanted to call Bobby by his name but couldn't recall it. Bobby felt that the old man on the stairs was trying to reach out to him and his mother in some way, to speak to them. But he couldn't.

That was the terribly sad thing.

The terribly wrong thing was that you could almost see right through this old man. Bobby was sure he could see the staircase through him, as if the old man were made of the same stuff as one of those cloud-sheep he had seen earlier that became thinner and thinner and more and more transparent as he looked.

Just for one second he thought the old man might be Daddy, because Daddy had suddenly started to look very old at breakfast yesterday. But it wasn't Daddy. It could have been. There was something in his face. But it wasn't. He thought he could almost hear the old man screeching inside his head – who am I who am I who are you tell me tell me tell me – and then his mother tugged him by the arm and said, 'Don't dawdle. Or we'll be late.'

Together they hurried out of the hotel door. The taxi was waiting and the driver was loading their cases into the boot. The heat and the blinding sunlight that met Bobby as he went outside dissolved the memory of the old man on the stairs. It was as if he had never been.

Theo

One

Plop!

The vicar of the church of St Joseph of Arimathea feels a drop of water strike his head, right where the hair has begun to thin, exposing the beginnings of a bald spot. He's halfway through his Sunday-morning sermon, for which he has chosen as his text Galatians VI. The drop of water makes him pause, look around the church for a second and lose his thread.

The front three rows are occupied. He knows the names of each member of the congregation as well as he knows his own. The same faces appear at every coffee morning, wine and cheese evening, and every other event that he and his wife Christine organise in the constant struggle to keep this church alive. There is deaf Mr Bell and his wife. Alan and Myra Johnson. Mike Graham, the church-warden. Old Miss McFarlane. They are all over sixty. If they have children or grandchildren, they never bring them. There are rarely any new faces. There are almost never children in the church, except at Christmas or for weddings or christenings, hauled in by their parents who turn up once and never appear again.

At the back of the church sits George, next to the door, his face in shadow. He never sits at the front.

And he always slips away before the service has ended, leaving a pound coin on the collection plate. He's shy. It's understandable.

The vicar gathers his wits and returns to his sermon. His pause has been so momentary that nobody has noticed. Sometimes he wonders how they would react if he simply got up and left in the middle of the service. Is Martha Taylor, sitting there in the front row clutching her hymn book, listening to a word he says? Or has ever said? It would be interesting to know.

Plop! Another drop strikes his head. He looks up. He can't help it. He peers up at the whitewashed vaulted ceiling above him and sees, spinning down towards him from an infinite distance, another drop of water, which smacks him lightly on the bridge of his nose. He raises his hand to his face to wipe away the moisture and continues his sermon.

His voice drones in the silent church, rises and falls as he tries to breathe some life into the words. What would the sixteen middle-aged or elderly men and women sitting in front of him think, if he were to suggest, 'Well, this is a terrible waste of time. Why don't we all go to the pub?'

But, of course, he would never say that, he would never even think of saying that, the words just popped into his mind. Maybe a demon put them there. He doesn't think so. He doesn't believe in demons. He doesn't believe in angels either.

Plop-plop-plop.

It is an unlooked-for baptism. The cold water trickles down his neck, moistening his collar. It runs down his forehead and then down his cheeks, so that it looks as if he is weeping. The drips increase in their frequency until they become a thin stream, as if someone up there has turned on a tap.

'We seem to have a leak in the roof,' the vicar says. Faces look up at him. They show no curiosity, no alarm. They show no emotion at all. They don't quite know what the vicar is talking about. A door bangs at the back of the church and then George comes down the aisle, his face averted, with a bucket that he's found in the vestry where the cleaning lady left it. He marches quickly up to the lectern and helps the vicar move it out of the way, then places the bucket underneath the leak in the roof. A moment later, he's disappeared once more into the shadows at the back of the church.

The vicar brings the sermon to an abrupt end and nods to the organist, who strikes the chords of the next hymn: 'How Cheering is the Christian's Hope'. A little later, he invites the congregation to take Communion. Everyone comes to the altar except, of course, George. The service draws to its conclusion. When the vicar walks back up the aisle, George has gone.

The vicar walks to the church door, inspecting the meagre contents of the collection plate as he passes it. He stands at the door of his church, still wearing his surplice, and shakes the hand of each member of his congregation as they shuffle homewards.

'Thank you for a nice service, vicar.'

'Lovely to see you. Will you be at the coffee morning next Saturday? Christine is so looking forward to seeing you.'

'Oh, yes. Wouldn't miss it.'

The departing churchgoers speed up as they leave the shelter of the church porch. Rain is falling steadily from a dull grey sky. Soon the last of them has disappeared through the gate that opens onto the lane below.

Mike Graham, a churchwarden, stays behind. He helps the vicar to lock everything away in the vestry and tidy up. Then they look at the bucket on the floor of the chancel. The drips are slowing down, but their point of origin is clearly visible in the large, circular damp patch on the ceiling.

'Are you thinking what I'm thinking, John?' asks Mike.

'We'd better go and look.'

They go outside. The rain has turned to a fine drizzle that wets their faces as they walk along the gravel path that leads around the church to the exterior walls of the chancel.

The church of St Joseph of Arimathea is not that old, though an ancient church once stood where the present building is situated. This building is constructed in the Gothic style, put up during the period of the Oxford movement in the mid-nineteenth century and funded by local mine owners. It must have been a handsome edifice when it was first used not quite two hundred years ago. The limestone it was built with was once honey-coloured, but is now darkened by acidic streaks so that it looks as if the church is made of soot. It stands on top of a hill, surrounded by a churchyard, with views across the valley.

From here on a clear day you can see down the Tyne Valley to the market town of Hexham. You can see the square tower of the abbey. The abbey was built over 1,300 years ago, part of the diocese of Lindisfarne, one of the very earliest places of Christian worship in Britain. Cuthbert, one of the first British saints, was a bishop here. In Hexham Abbey there is a sense of a magical connection back to the earliest times in the history of Christianity. There is no such sense of connection in St Joseph's.

And looking north from the hill on which St Joseph's stands, you can see the ridge along which runs Hadrian's Wall. Built in the second century, a few of its mile castles and forts still survive and there are sections of the wall itself standing here and there along its eighty-mile course that have somehow escaped being plundered for their dressed stones. There's hardly a building of any age in this part of the world that does not have stone from the Roman Wall in it. Even the foundations of St Joseph's are Roman stone. Directly below the church are the wet slate roofs and smoking chimneys of the small town it serves.

The churchwarden and the vicar back off a little from the path, standing in the grass and weeds that encroach upon the gravestones in order to peer up at the roof of the church.

'Oh God,' says Mike.

'Bastards,' says the vicar.

Somebody's been on the roof and has ripped off a long section of lead flashing that lined a gully. The whole area is badly damaged. Slates are broken or have been thrown onto the ground below. There's hardly a roof there at all. They walk forward again and inspect the gravel.

'They had a ladder here,' says Mike, pointing to two indentations in the path.

'Vandals,' says John Elliott, his heart bursting with rage. The veins on his neck swell, and his face reddens. If one of the perpetrators had been in front of them right now, his life might have been in danger.

Mike gets out a mobile phone, takes pictures. 'That's going to cost us,' he says. 'I'll call the police.'

'Thousands of pounds,' agrees John. 'And for what? A few hundred pounds'-worth of lead?'

'They say it goes to China.'

Mike calls the police while the vicar walks up and down the path.

'They can't spare anyone at present,' says Mike, after a brief conversation on his mobile. 'They're busy. They've got my number.'

'Bastards,' says the vicar again. It isn't clear whether he means the vandals who took the lead or the police, who obviously have better things to do than come to the scene of this particular crime.

'It must have happened last night,' says Mike.

'I'll contact the insurers. We'd better get some plastic sheeting up there until it can be fixed.'

'I've got a friend who's a builder,' says Mike. 'I'll call him. He's probably in the pub right now.'

The vicar remembers his random thought earlier on about taking everyone to the pub. He has a mental picture of the inside of a pub late on a Sunday morning: cheerful people jostling to get to the bar, laughter and fellowship and conversation as everyone gets a pint or two inside them before going home for the Sunday roast.

He wishes he was with them.

Two

Christine is cooking Sunday lunch when he returns home. Home is a small, detached house on the hillside below the church, built on the site of a much larger Victorian vicarage that once stood there. The original vicarage has been pulled down and the grounds have been developed as a housing estate. The vicar and his wife live in one of the new houses. It is built so badly that when the wind comes from the south-west, it feels as if it is blowing straight through the house. None of the windows fit properly. The pointing is already crumbling, even though the house is only a few years old, and damp patches appear on the bedroom walls when it rains.

'How did it go?' asks Christine.

'Same as usual. Less than twenty in church. What's for lunch?'

'Chicken.'

The vicar has to go out again in the early afternoon, to pursue one of his many and varied duties that never cease, even on a Sunday afternoon. Chicken is a lot cheaper than sirloin or a leg of lamb. The vicar can't remember the last time they ate a joint of roast beef.

'Someone's stolen the lead flashing from the church roof,' he tells Christine, coming into the kitchen as she is basting the chicken.

'Oh no!'

'It will cost thousands to repair.'

'How could anybody do such a thing?'

'I don't know.'

John Elliott goes to the fridge, takes out a can of beer and pops it open. He pours it into a glass and sits at the kitchen table. Indeed, he doesn't know. He doesn't know anything any more. He doesn't know why he goes on with a job that he no longer enjoys, struggling to preserve a church that most people in the town have turned away from. If you stopped someone in the streets and asked for directions to St Joseph's, chances are they wouldn't be quite sure how to get there. Chances are that one or two people you stopped might never even have heard of the church.

John Elliott doesn't look particularly ecclesiastical when he takes his dog collar off. He's just under six foot, square-shouldered and solidly built, with dark hair cut short and a ruddy face: the complexion of someone who has always spent a great deal of his life out of doors.

He was born in the Scottish Borders, in the town of Hawick. His father was a minister in the Church of Scotland. He grew up in a family where God and rugby were the two important things in life. His father was a respected man in the community and had once been a promising rugby player himself. His father's religion and his occupation in the church meant the house was always full: members of the congregation calling in for cups of coffee, to discuss their personal woes or else the prospects for 'The Greens' – as the local rugby club was known – that season. His father's love of sport meant that John Elliott devoted most of his weekends to playing rugby. He became a promising member of a junior team, and was spoken of as a candidate for playing in the Borders Cup in a few years' time, if life had gone right for them all.

Life didn't go right for the Elliott family. When he was just sixteen, his father sickened and died. There was almost no warning: that is to say, his father and mother concealed his father's illness from John and his sister Karen until almost the last moment. Then, at the young age of fifty, Charles Elliott went into hospital and never came out again alive.

The effect on the family was dramatic. The house they lived in was the property of the diocese and had to be made available to whoever would become Charles Elliott's successor. John Elliott's mother Helen couldn't face life in Hawick without her husband. Without consulting her children, she decided to move back to Alnwick in Northumberland, her home town, where she had a cousin with a house large enough to accommodate her and her two children.

John Elliott's life could have gone in a different direction if the family had stayed in Hawick. He had felt no special leaning towards the Church at the time his father died. He wasn't even sure he shared his father's faith, while accepting that his father had done a good job as a minister. If his world had not been turned upside down so suddenly, it is probable he might have become a trainee accountant or solicitor. Or else, he could have got a job working as an auctioneer at the Mart. Those were the sorts of careers his friends were pursuing as the time approached when they would leave school. But it wasn't to be.

John felt a weight of guilt on his shoulders when his father died. He blamed himself for not noticing that his father was ill, for not spending more time with him and for continuing to give him the sort of worries that all teenage children give their parents. He was too busy enjoying life. He shouldn't have blamed himself when his father died, but he did. When his mother decided to move south, back into England, he saw her misery and her loneliness and told himself that the only way to make her happy again would be for him to follow in his father's footsteps and dedicate his life to the Church, even if it was a different church, the Church of England.

His belief, or his lack of it, didn't seem to be an obstacle. His own observations of his father's profession led him to the conclusion that being a minister, or a vicar, was mostly about community work. He had no objections to that.

He was never an academic child, but he worked hard at his new school in Alnwick and managed to stay on to do his A levels. And his life didn't just consist of studying. Before he left the Borders, he'd met a girl at a rugby club dance – Christine Johnstone was her name. He'd liked her, and he'd liked her parents, Charlie and Rose, who lived on the edge of Kelso, a town about twenty miles from Hawick. He kept in touch with her even after they moved south of the border.

Then, against all expectations, he won a place at the University of Durham to study theology. Now he had to decide whether working in the Church really was his vocation. He persuaded himself that it was. He convinced himself that his optimism was strong enough to over-come any difficulty. His enthusiasm infected his tutors and lecturers, and persuaded the Bishops' Advisory Panel of his fitness to become an ordinand. He trained in parishes in small industrial towns up and down the North-East coast, learning a little about the hard side of his future job.

At last he was ordained and, in his early thirties, a plum of a job fell into his lap. That's how it seemed at the time, anyway.

The incumbent of St Joseph's had had a nervous breakdown and – just at that moment – there was no obvious successor. There were plenty of other clergymen who would have liked the job, but somehow John Elliott's name had caught the bishop's eye and he was offered the position. He'd been going out with Christine for years by that stage and now he could offer her a house and the security of a regular salary. They married in Kelso; the wedding party took place on a sunny day in May in the garden of a pub looking out across the Tweed. The river was silver in the sunshine. The two families, John's old friends from his Hawick days, and some of his new ones from south of the border, gathered on the lawn and sipped pints of beer.

John very often looks back on that day as the happiest day of his life. His new wife looking pretty in her wedding dress, all five foot four of her. His mother bursting into tears every few minutes, and then smiling damply to show that she too is happy. His friends are all around him, and there's lots of banter. His old coach from the rugby club gives a short but pithy speech that has everyone in fits of laughter. His tutor from Durham University has taken the day off to see him get married. A good day, even if his father was not there to see it. The world was at his feet.

His new parish, where he would take up residency after the honeymoon in Greece that Christine's parents had paid for, would be a blank slate upon which he could write the story of his life. It would be a story of hope for other parishes: John Elliott would show what could be achieved by hard work and a vigorous faith. He would fill the church with a congregation of young and old alike. It would reverberate to the sound of many voices. He would raise money to repair it and clean it and paint it: the old building badly needed attention. He would promote the work of the Church throughout his parish.

It hasn't quite worked out like that. His wedding day – so clear, so bright in his memory – remains the landmark day of his life because the days that have followed it, seven or eight hundred of them, are less and less satisfactory. The days that he is living through now, as another Christmas draws near, sometimes feel to him as dark as the skies on this wet and gusty Sunday.

It's not his marriage. His marriage is a rock in a stormy sea. Christine is sensible and down to earth and keeps her husband from overindulging in self-accusation. She may be small, but she's full of energy. She's a teacher at the Temple School, the local primary, and is well thought of, she makes friends easily. That they have a social life at all is mainly due to Christine. Although John Elliott doesn't see it himself, he's becoming morose.

He thinks he's a failure, that's the problem. All of the goals he set himself when he took on the living of St Joseph's remain just that; goals, further away now than on the day he first arrived here.

He thinks it must be his fault when his parishioners tell him they're too busy to come to church on Sunday. 'Our lad plays football on Sunday mornings.' 'My husband works most Saturdays, Sunday's the only day we can do our shopping.' 'I'll come next week if I can.' He's heard all the excuses. Mostly people don't even bother to explain. They just stare at him and say, 'Nah, I've better things to do with my weekend.'

The only people he can persuade to come to his services are the frail, who want to get on the right side of God, if there is a God, before it's too late; the terminally bored, who will go anywhere and do anything to see another human being for a few minutes every week; and George. George's reasons for coming to the church aren't clear, but John Elliott doesn't want to ask him, in case he decides to stop coming and the congregation shrinks from seventeen to sixteen. The same sixteen people who have been coming, week after week, since the previous vicar left.

He knows that some of the churches in the valley still have full congregations. Sometimes he wonders if it's the place itself – as if somehow the air at St Joseph's is exhausted, as if all the oxygen in it has somehow been consumed, leaving nothing to nourish the flame of belief he feels it is his duty to preserve.

John Elliott's marriage is what keeps him sane. Christine loves her job as a primary-school teacher; it helps with the money and it keeps her busy. She loves children. She'd love a child of her own too, but so far they haven't been blessed. John wants a son more than anything, and sometimes he prays that God will give them a break, that God will direct his eager spermatozoa to the most fertile ovum, that this collision will form a zygote, that the zygote will become an embryo, that the embryo will become a bright, healthy young boy, quick on his feet and a natural scrum half.

But they haven't been blessed. Not yet.

Christine slaps a plate down in front of him. 'You haven't been listening to a word I've been saying,' she says, in an exasperated tone he's becoming used to. That's his fault too: sometimes he doesn't listen to a word she says because he finds it too easy to get bound up in his thoughts.

131

'I'm sorry,' he replies. 'I was wool-gathering.'

'I said, I've been given Joanna Dixon's class. Year Five.'

'Why, what's happened to her?'

'Maternity leave. I told you.'

'What are they like?' asks John Elliott.

'You'll see. I want you to come and help me on Wednesday afternoon. There's an indoor football game I'm to supervise, and I don't know the rules.'

'Won't your headmistress mind?'

'No,' Christine tells him. 'As long as you don't start lecturing them about God. She's very keen not to offend the parents of children brought up in other faiths.'

Christine's voice has a note of sarcasm. The headmistress of the Temple School is known for her up-to-date views.

The two of them sit and eat their roast chicken in silence. Then Christine says, 'You're not much fun to be with these days.'

'Am I not?' replies John. 'I'm sorry.'

'Do you have to go out this afternoon? We have so little time together at weekends.'

'Unfortunately I do. I've promised to go and visit Alfred Stone.'

Christine has to be reminded of who Alfred Stone is: the former vicar of St Joseph's.

'Oh, he's the one who's in St Mark's.'

St Mark's is a hospital which houses a low to medium-secure unit for the long-term care of the mentally unwell.

'That's right. He hasn't been well enough to have visitors for a long time, but they promised to ring me if he recovered sufficiently, and I got the call yesterday. So I feel I ought to go.'

132

John Elliott leaves home half an hour later and drives in his Nissan Note towards the sad towns of the North-East littoral, where old colliery villages have either been abandoned or else have morphed into housing estates for commuters working in Newcastle. Sandwiched between a huge corrugated metal barn selling second-hand cars and a retail park, he finds the Victorian building that is home to the Reverend Alfred Stone.

The hospital, which was built by private subscription in the 1880s, looks from the outside as if it belongs on the seafront in Bournemouth: a stranded Grand Hotel that has washed up amongst this wilderness of metal sheds. Inside the lighting is harsh, the place smells of fresh paint and the floors are green lino. He makes his way to the ward where Alfred Stone is staying and finds a nurse.

'He's in the TV lounge,' she tells him. 'At least, that's where he was five minutes ago. I'll go and find him.'

She returns in a moment.

'He's gone back to his room. I'll take you. Who did you say you were?'

John Elliott explains.

'Only he's still a bit nervous about visitors. Here we are. Don't stay too long. He's been doing so well, and we don't want to overtire him and have a relapse now, do we, my duck?'

These last words are addressed to a frail-looking man in his sixties. He is in his pyjamas and sitting up in bed. A pale face, watery-blue eyes and a beaky nose and thin lips are framed by grey hair which has been allowed to grow too long, so that it curls over the collar of his pyjama jacket.

He hasn't shaved for a day or two. He sits with the pillows plumped up behind his head and looks at John Elliott with apprehension. Outside, the grey cloud has parted for a moment and a square of sunlight falls on the counterpane.

It is more a cubicle than a room. Apart from a radio and a dressing gown hung on the back of the door, there are few personal possessions. There are no cards or flowers on the bedside table, and no books or magazines in view. John Elliott wonders what this man does with himself. Has he been in his pyjamas for the last two years? And how does he kill the time?

He introduces himself and is relieved to see that there is no confusion in the man's eyes.

'Ah yes,' he says. 'You wrote to me. That was very kind.'

'I'm sorry I haven't been to see you before. The hospital said you weren't receiving visitors.'

'I've been very busy. But how nice to meet you.'

Alfred Stone's voice is hoarse and tremulous, as if he can't quite get enough air into his lungs. He doesn't explain what has kept him so busy, but with a graceful motion of one hand indicates a chair beside the bed.

John Elliott sits down. The nurse, who has waited in the room to see that all is well, turns to leave, but Alfred Stone calls after her in his quavering voice: 'Nurse, my visitor might like a cup of tea. Would you be awfully kind and see if the tea trolley is anywhere about?'

He speaks to her as if she is a domestic servant waiting on him in his vicarage. The nurse doesn't seem put out.

'I expect Dora will bring the trolley round in a moment.'

She leaves and Alfred puts his hand on John Elliott's arm and says in a stage whisper, 'The staff here are terribly nice, but the service isn't always what you and I would wish for.'

'How are you?' says John Elliott in the cheerful voice that he cultivates for home visits to the sick and needy.

'I'm very well,' says Alfred. He sounds like a man of eighty, although John Elliott knows he has just turned sixty. 'And you, dear boy? How are you enjoying St Joseph's?'

'I'm only sorry that I acquired the position as a result of your ill health.'

'But you are enjoying working in the parish?' Alfred persists. John Elliott smiles meaninglessly and is saved from further inquisition by the rattle of crockery. Dora has arrived. Their conversation is interrupted for a moment by Dora's cheerful chatter as she pours two mugs of tea. They sip their tea. John Elliott can't think of anything else to say, but Alfred Stone has a question he needs to ask. 'Tell me, are you a Christian?'

John is confused for a moment. He answers, 'Well, as you know, I'm an ordained priest like you.'

Alfred Stone gives a crafty smile. 'That won't do, you know. Do you believe in the Resurrection? Do you believe Jesus really died and went to hell, then came back to life three days later?'

There's only one way to go in a conversation like this. John Elliott has to humour this man. The alternative is to leave. He replies in as neutral a voice as possible: 'Of course I do. There may be some debate to be had about the historical facts and the record in the Gospels, but the symbolic truth of the Resurrection is beyond doubt. Of course I believe in it.'

Alfred Stone says, 'I belong – or should I say, I belonged – to what you might call the modernising wing of our Church. I believed in the ordination of women bishops. I believed in the ordination of gay priests. I believed in the God that was created by the Church of England – an elderly and vigorous God, wearing a cardigan, with liberal views and a great supporter of the Royal Family. I didn't believe that at the Last Supper the wine really did turn into blood.'

He seems a little excited now, and his fingers have begun to pluck at his bedspread. John Elliott says pacifically: 'Perhaps now is not the moment to worry about how literal the scriptures are. Sacramental Union is what we are taught, isn't it?'

'But now *is* the moment. If not now, when? With whom can I share my thoughts, if not a fellow priest?'

Alfred Stone stops speaking and begins to weep. John Elliott is shocked. He stands up. 'I'm troubling you. I should go.'

'No. *Don't go.*'

The last two words are hissed rather than spoken. John Elliott sits down again. He doesn't know what to do. Perhaps he should ring for the nurse.

'Don't go,' repeats Alfred Stone. 'Not now.' He's calmer again. He smears the moisture from his cheeks with the back of his hand. 'I'm all right. Just a little overtired. I think too much, the doctors tell me. But how can I stop myself thinking, even to please them? Have you had the dreams yet?'

'Dreams? What dreams?' asks John Elliott. It is clear to him that the former vicar of St Joseph's has a long road to travel before he will be well enough to leave this place.

'If you need to ask, then they haven't started. When they do, come and see me again. Then we'll talk some more.'

'Would it help you if we prayed together?' asks John Elliott. Alfred Stone begins to laugh, then checks himself.

'Pray to whom? To the modern God of our modernising Church? You're just like I was. You don't really believe in any of it. You don't believe that the essence of Christ inhabits the wine and the wafers at Communion. You believe in the value of a Christian way of life, and you might imagine some sort of afterlife, but I'm sure you don't believe that there is a place where God sits on his throne surrounded by cherubim and seraphim. And I'm sure you don't believe that Christ descended into hell before his Resurrection. You probably don't even believe there *is* such a place as hell. You don't believe in demons. You don't believe that Beelzebub and Apollyon have ever existed, or ever could exist. I'm sure you're a good man and do good work. But you don't know the half of it.'

'The half of what?'

Alfred Stone looks around the room as if to ensure they aren't being overheard. Then he leans closer to John Elliott as if he wishes to impart a great confidence.

'*What if it is all true*? You hadn't thought about that, had you? What if there are such things as angels, with their great, black wings? What if there is such a place as hell, so near to us that sometimes we can feel the scorch of its flames and smell the sulphur from its pits?'

The nurse appears in the doorway. By now, Alfred Stone is sitting bolt upright in his bed, the veins on his neck standing out like cords, his pale face blotched with scarlet. His voice rings out like a church bell, not shaky any more but so loud it must be audible throughout the ward.

'*What if it is all true*?' he shouts.

'Oh dear,' says the nurse mildly. 'He's getting excited. We'll have to give him something to calm him down. I'm afraid you'd better leave.'

John Elliott looks at her gratefully and gets to his feet. He hadn't bargained for any of this. He can do no good here. As he turns to leave, Alfred Stone calls after him, 'So good of you to look in on me, dear boy. Do call again soon. And next time I'll tell you what I saw one night a few years ago. *At St Joseph's.*'

Outside it is cool and rainy. John Elliott feels as if he has been underground for the last year and, as he emerges, he breathes in the fresh and chilly air until his lungs are full. When he finds his car, he has to sit for a moment in the driver's seat before he feels ready to switch on the engine.

Are you a Christian? What kind of a question is that for one priest to ask another? He's sorry he came. He thinks he has probably done more harm than good. He thinks he could have spent his Sunday afternoon with Christine, instead of wasting it on this fruitless expedition. Why's he worrying about some semi-lunatic when it's quite clear his own wife needs some love and attention? Where is his sense of his priorities? It's a while before his hands are steady enough for him to start the drive back to St Joseph's.

Three

On Wednesday afternoon, John Elliott goes to the Temple School where Christine works. It was once a church school before it was handed over to the local education authority. But the connection has been forgotten. In the early days of his tenure, John Elliott sent a message to the school through Christine, offering his assistance with the Easter play. The headmistress replied in a letter.

Dear Mr Elliott,

Christine tells me you were so kind as to offer your help with our Easter play. I'm afraid we have very clear policies on cultural, ethnic and religious diversity in this school. A play that celebrates a purely Christian vision of our past might cause offence to some parents and would not conform to the policy as stated above. We will, as usual, be putting on a play at the end of Spring term, but the theme this year will be a talent contest . . .

The Temple School is in a small town in the heart of rural Northumberland. There are three young girls there whose father, Siddiq Khan, is a local car dealer and whose ethnicity is Indo-Aryan. There is a Chinese boy whose father runs a takeaway. The rest of the children are mostly the sons and daughters of local farmers and shopkeepers, accountants and solicitors.

When he arrives at the school, John Elliott heads for the gym, a new block to one side of the main school building. There he finds Christine, looking fetching in football shorts and a baggy jersey, blowing hard on a whistle in an attempt to get the attention of twenty or so small boys and girls. The gym has the usual equipment of bars and ropes, and a composite floor that is not too hard if you fall over. The children are all between nine or ten years old and have a great deal of energy. There is noise and confusion and giggling, but after a while Christine and her husband manage to restore order. John explains the rules of football in as much detail as he thinks is necessary. He suspects some of the boys already know a great deal more about it than he does, but they all listen politely.

Two teams are chosen. Two portable goal nets have been set up at each end of the gym. John Elliott strides into the middle of the floor holding a football. He drops it on the ground and blows a whistle to mark the start of the game. There is immediate chaos with small girls and boys darting in every direction, the ball rolling around between them. Voices rise in pleas and complaints and laughter.

'Sir, sir, Eric was offside, wasn't he? Sir, please, sir?'

'Rachel pushed me over. It's not fair.'

Christine and John Elliott deal with these objections in a summary way. A small boy of about nine, dark-haired, kicks the football into his own team's goal and shouts, 'Yay!'

'That's our goal, you idiot!' shouts the boy next to him.

'Own goal! Own goal!' chant the members of the opposite team.

'Theo, you're supposed to kick it into the goal at the other end, not this one,' explains Christine. The boy gives a rueful shrug and smiles.

'I forgot,' is all he says. The other children don't appear to be cross with him.

'Typical Theo!' someone shouts, but the remark is not unkind.

The game goes on. After forty minutes, everyone is flagging and it is time for the football to end. The children stream off to the changing rooms and Christine goes with them.

'I'll see you outside,' says John Elliott.

'No need to wait. This lot have finished for the afternoon, but I've got to stay on for a staff meeting.'

John Elliott goes outside. It is a bright November afternoon, the sun already low in a blue sky streaked with white cirrus clouds. The sky is clear enough to suggest that there will be a frost tonight. Autumn is coming to an end, the last few brown leaves fluttering to the ground. The days are getting shorter. The shadows will be lengthening in the Church of St Joseph of Arimathea, the bars of sunlight shining through its windows streaked with the blue and red of the stained glass. The church will be cold, and with each day, as the winter draws nearer, the cold will sink deeper into the stone floors and pillars.

Outside the school gates, parents are beginning to gather, and school taxis have parked nearby to transport the children who live beyond the town limits to the little upland villages on the edge of the moors or under the shadow of Kielder Forest.

He's in no hurry. In half an hour, he's meeting the loss assessor from the insurance company at the church, to talk about the cost of repairing the roof. He looks at the children's mothers standing in little groups of two and three, chatting amongst themselves as they wait for their children. None of them have ever been to his church, as far as he knows. He envies them. They worry about their mortgages and their credit-card bills and the cost of their holidays and their children's clothes, but they don't have the dead weight of a cold and empty church upon their shoulders. They don't know what it's like to beg and scrimp and save money from collection plates and bring-and-buy sales and coffee mornings, all in order to meet the Parish Share, to preserve a stone building that stands empty most of the time.

Already some of the children have changed, and are racing past John Elliott to meet their parents. Then Christine is beside him, asking, 'What time will you be home?'

'About five? I have a meeting with the loss assessor now.'

She heads back towards the school buildings and John Elliott walks through the school gates towards his car. A small boy rushes past him. It's Theo, who scored a goal against his own side. His mother – it can only be his mother, the same dark hair, the same oval face as her son – is standing on her own a few yards from the other parents. She's not one of them. She makes no effort to talk to anyone, her eyes only on the small boy who is now approaching her. He hurries over to her and takes her hand but, as John Elliott walks past the two of them, Theo turns towards him and says, 'Goodbye, Mr Elliott. Thank you for the football game.'

John Elliott is surprised that the child has remembered his name, surprised too that he has bothered to acknowledge him and to thank him. The mother glances at the vicar and smiles. There's something in her smile that makes John Elliott wonder if she is hiding some sadness. But her face is very calm. With a slight shock, he realises she's rather beautiful. How come he's never noticed her on any of his previous visits to the school? He'll recognise her the next time he sees her. Mother and son are smiling together, and then they turn away and start walking down the hill. As he watches them go, he hears a voice in his ear, so close he almost jumps.

'Good afternoon, vicar. Have you been ministering to the children?'

It's George. John Elliott is surprised to see him here. He didn't hear his approach. George is wearing a flat cap, a full-length waterproof coat and wellington boots. He has black leather gloves on his hands. He looks as if he's dressed for an expedition.

'No, not at all. My wife teaches here and I've been helping to organise a game of football. What about you? Do you have children?'

As John Elliott asks this question, he realises how ridiculous it sounds. He's never seen George with anybody else, and the idea of George being a father and having children just doesn't seem probable. George gives his odd, sideways smile when the vicar says this and answers, 'No, vicar, I'm a bachelor. I've never seemed to appeal to the female of the species. I can't think why.'

This remark – an oblique reference to George's unfortunate appearance – is typical of George. It is obviously designed to make the vicar feel uncomfortable, and it does.

'I do like watching children play,' adds George. 'Don't worry, vicar, I'm not some disgusting old paedo. It's just that I didn't have much of a childhood myself. You might

143

say I didn't have a childhood at all. It was a very solitary existence. But I like watching children play and seeing, second-hand, what childhood is all about. If only I could paint, I would love to capture it on canvas. But, unfortunately, my talents lie in other directions.'

He doesn't specify what talents these are. For a moment the two of them contemplate the children streaming out of the school, laughing and jostling each other. The vicar never knows when George is being serious, or when he's being sardonic. He's never understood George since he first met him.

'Well, I must be getting on,' says George. Places to go, people to see.'

He walks swiftly down the hill in the direction of the town centre.

George's voice is thin, high-pitched and cultivated, without any trace of a Geordie or a Northumbrian accent. The vicar doesn't know where he comes from, but he's not local. A few months ago, George started turning up for Sunday services at St Joseph's. He was the last to appear and always left before the vicar could speak to him. But one morning he did stay behind, and seemed keen to talk to the vicar, waiting until everyone else had left. After he had introduced himself, George had said, 'Might I ask you a great favour?'

'If I can be of any help, I will.'

'I wonder,' George had asked, 'if I might trouble you to write a letter on my behalf to the county council. A character reference, so to speak. It's in connection with a business venture I am setting up.'

The vicar had hesitated. 'Well, I'm not quite sure what I'd say. Today's the first time we've ever spoken, isn't it?'

George had given him a look. His deformity made it hard to tell, but the vicar thought it was a smile.

'Just so, vicar. All I ask is that you say that I'm a regular member of your congregation.'

The vicar hesitated again, and George added, 'I promise I will continue to come here every Sunday even after you've written the letter. You'll be sick of the sight of me before I'm finished.'

It was a promise; perhaps also intended as a joke at his own expense. The vicar couldn't see a way out. To refuse would be downright rude to someone whom an accident of birth, no fault of his own, had made physically unappealing. He agreed to write a letter in those terms. He handed it over to George the following Sunday, feeling slightly uneasy that he was endorsing the character of a stranger, and doubting that he would ever see George again. In this, he was wrong. That was over a year ago and George hasn't missed a Sunday morning since then; indeed, he'd made himself useful by helping to distribute the church newsletter and in other small ways as well.

But he is still an enigma as far as the vicar is concerned. John Elliott walks to his car, and goes off to the meeting with the loss assessor.

That evening, he asks Christine: 'Have you met Theo's mother yet?'

'Not really, not to speak to. Why?'

'I saw her at the school gates. I thought she looked rather . . .'

He pauses for a moment. Rather what? Why is he thinking about her, and her son? He finds that he has been. They've been in his head all afternoon, without him knowing it. Christine answers for him. 'She looks rather lonely, if that's what you mean. She doesn't mix with the other mothers, not as far as I've seen.'

'What's the father like?'

Christine pauses for a second, then says, 'Actually, I don't know about the father. She lives with a partner. Theo calls him Geordie, but he's not Theo's father. I think Mary Constantine was separated from Theo's real father, and then hooked up with this Geordie person about a year ago. I don't know anything about him either. The boy's sweet.'

Then they talk of other things.

That night, John Elliott can't settle in his bed. He keeps turning over and rearranging the duvet and scratching his head until, at last, Christine switches on her bedside lamp and says, 'Oh, for God's sake. What's the matter with you?'

'Sorry. I don't know. Something's bothering me.'

'Well, try and be bothered a bit more quietly.'

John Elliott lies in his bed as straight as a poker, trying not to move a muscle. He gets cramp in his toes. His nose starts to itch. There's something not right: something to do with his church. He sits bolt upright in bed and Christine mutters thickly, but he can't make out the words.

He gets out of bed quietly and whispers, 'I'm just going to check on the church. I've a feeling those vandals might be out and about tonight.'

No answer, just a small snore. He pads across the room to where his clothes have been thrown on a chair and slips on his trousers and a shirt and carries his shoes downstairs. By the front door a fleece is hanging up. He puts it on, and hunts around for a torch. He finds one in the kitchen, then quietly leaves the house.

Outside it's very cold. A frost glitters in the starlight on bushes and trees. The windows of his car are white. The sky is very clear and bright with stars. John Elliott looks up and sees millions of them, more than he ever imagined existed in the night sky. In truth, the vandals who stole the lead from his church roof are not the cause of his wakefulness. It's something else: a feeling at the back of his mind like a fingernail scraping on a blackboard. He turns into the steep lane that leads up to St Joseph's. The starlight is so bright that he doesn't need to switch on his torch. He comes to the gate that opens into the church-yard, and pauses. If there are vandals up there, he had better be careful. Of course he's forgotten his mobile. It's still on the kitchen table. He listens, but hears no sounds.

Or does he? He thinks for a moment that he can hear someone murmuring words that he can't quite make out. Then he decides it is the sudden wind that has got up from nowhere, and is sighing around the church. He glances up at the sky and, far above, sees the black edge of a cloud that has begun to occlude the stars.

He walks carefully up the path towards the church. On either side of him is an avenue of low, clipped yew bushes. Beyond those lie the gravestones of two centuries or more. Some are upright; some lie flat. A few are ornamented with small statues – stone cherubs and the like. He can make out the silhouette of a larger statue in a far corner, almost life-size. He stops. He doesn't remember any such statue in his churchyard.

He clicks on his torch. But nothing happens. He can't understand why. He *knows* he put a new battery in there on Monday, the day after he discovered the hole in the church roof, and he hasn't used the torch since then.

147

The wind moans about the church and the sky above him is darkening, as more clouds fill from the north. There's someone standing in his churchyard, amongst the gravestones, in the middle of the night.

'Hello,' he calls in a hesitant voice. 'Is there anybody there?'

He's shivering, and not just from the cold. The black silhouette moves, and then it's walking towards him. For a moment he feels an unreasonable fear, but what's he afraid of? Some tramp? He can deal with that.

It isn't a tramp. As the figure comes closer, he sees that it is a woman. She too sounds nervous when she speaks. 'Who is it?' she asks.

He doesn't recognise the voice but, a moment later, she is close enough for him to make out her features. He's seen her before, earlier that same day, waiting outside the school for her son Theo.

'It's John Elliott,' he replies. 'The vicar. I'm sorry if I startled you.'

She says, 'I hope you don't mind me being here.'

He's struggling to remember her name. Christine mentioned it only a few hours ago. Mary Constantine, that's it.

'You're Theo's mother.'

She's instantly on her guard. She steps back a pace. 'How do you know Theo?'

'My wife, Christine, is his teacher. I helped her organise a game of football at the school this afternoon, and Theo was there. He scored a goal.'

Mary Constantine doesn't drop her guard, or acknowledge the vicar's explanation in any way.

'Well, I'd better be getting home,' she says, as if the two of them have just met outside a shop in the town

148

and not at midnight in a churchyard. Something catches John Elliott's eye: a single snowflake, whirling down out of nowhere on the rising wind.

'It's starting to snow,' he says, looking up as a few more flakes appear. Some of them settle in Mary Constantine's dark hair and on her shoulders. They glisten like diamonds. 'I'm sorry to be so inquisitive, but what on earth are you doing freezing to death in a churchyard in the middle of the night?'

'I visit sometimes,' she replies. 'I have for years. You're the first person I've ever met here. That's why I come at night, so I don't meet people. I can think about things here. I ought to be getting on home, before Geordie or Theo wake up and notice I'm not there. Goodnight, vicar.'

The snow is falling more thickly now and the black clouds have covered most of the sky. The ground is so cold that the snow doesn't melt, but settles.

'You're welcome to come in the daytime too,' John Elliott tells her as she brushes past him and walks towards the gate. 'It would be lovely to see you in church sometime.'

She doesn't answer, or even turn her head, and in a moment she is lost to sight. It is much darker now that the stars are hidden and John Elliott tries his torch again. This time it works and in its beam he sees flakes of snow spinning down, whirling in a dance around the gravestones where Mary Constantine was standing a few moments before.

Four

During the night, moist air from the North Sea has driven inshore, and as it encounters the frigid cold over the land, snow flurries have started to fall. The next morning the streets of the little town are white and the air is arctic. People are out scraping their driveways and clearing car windscreens of their white burden. People are stamping their shoes and snorting clouds of vapour and making the remarks people always make when it snows.

'A bit sharp for November, vicar? Think it will last?'

'Aye, it's brass monkeys, isn't it?'

'Once it starts snowing like this, it'll forget to stop.'

The vicar acknowledges these remarks with a wave of his hand and a cheery smile. He doesn't know if it will last. Nor would it surprise him if this weather lasted until Judgement Day. He's cold, and it's not just the falling temperatures.

The whole county is struggling with the early arrival of winter. The high roads across the hills, into Scotland and down into Yorkshire and Cumbria, are all blocked. The sun comes out for a while and thaws the top few centimetres of the lying snow. Then clouds scud in on a bitter north-easterly and fresh showers cover the refrozen drifts. Soon the whole town is like a skating rink. The vicar parks his car at the bottom of the hill leading up to his house; it can't cope with the steep approach and just slides everywhere. Christine walks to school and falls over twice on the way.

As the weekend approaches, the weather, if anything, worsens. This is unexpected: even here, in the northernmost county in England, lying snow is uncommon before Christmas. There's still a month to go, and not only is there no thaw: the snow accumulates on roads, on fields and dyke-backs, on the frozen branches of trees. Every few hours, fresh showers blow in from the North Sea. The vicar finds that walking up the lane to St Joseph's is becoming like an Alpine ascent. At times he has to cling to the stone wall that borders the lane in order just to stay upright. On Saturday he phones his parishioners – the faithful who attend every Sunday without fail – to warn them not to attempt to come to church the following morning unless conditions improve. He doesn't want to have to worry about one of his congregation falling and breaking a hip.

Sunday comes around, and now his conscience won't let him lie in late, much as he'd like to. It is a grey and bitter day outside, a few flakes in the wind, but really too cold for persistent snow. Christine says, 'Why on earth can't you relax, just for once, and stay at home?'

It's a good question. Why can't he? He can't, because he thinks he's let himself and his employer down – and God, if there is a God. He has failed to fill the church. His congregation never grows. If he were a small business with this number of customers, he'd have closed the doors long ago. So that's why he has to be there. Even if he's the only person in the church, he has to be there. It's in his contract. He's a priest, and it's Sunday. He tries to explain this to Christine, but she tells him he's being bloody-minded and turns over in bed and pretends to go to sleep.

He puts on his coat and a scarf and sticks his shoes in his coat pockets. He slips on his wellington boots and plods carefully up the lane to the church. He unlocks the door and lets himself in. Inside the church it's like a cold store. He flicks on the lights and then turns on two underpowered blow heaters to try to produce the illusion of warmth. He has some idea of performing the morning service on his own, but now he's here it seems ridiculous. Is he really going to put on his surplice and perform his rites in an empty church?

But it's not an empty church for much longer. As he stands there wondering what to do, the door creaks open. George comes in, looks around the church and says, 'Just you and me today, is it, vicar? Well, when the going gets tough, the tough get going.'

The vicar looks at him. 'You want me to conduct a service?'

'That's why we're here, isn't it?' asks George. The vicar wonders if he can detect irony, but George's expression is deadpan.

'You can omit the hymns and some of the readings if you like,' says George. 'I won't mind. My singing voice is not my best feature.' He doesn't say what his best feature might be. Once again, the vicar thinks, George is using his disfigurement as a smokescreen. He acts the part well. Sometimes the vicar thinks he can glimpse an entirely different person behind the facade.

So John Elliott puts on his surplice, carries the cup and the wafers up to the altar, and lights the candles. George seats himself in his usual place at the back of the church.

'Won't you at least come and sit nearer the front?' the vicar asks him.

A voice from the darkness replies, 'I'm very comfortable here. You carry on. Don't mind me.'

And so John Elliott begins to conduct the Sunday-morning Communion service to an empty church: because even with George in it, it's empty. It's emptier with him in it than if he hadn't been there at all.

When he reaches that part of the service where the congregation is invited to join him, the vicar turns and looks at George. George doesn't budge. He's not going to make this easier. So the vicar drinks the wine and nibbles the wafer and speaks aloud the words of Invitation and Communion. Then he turns to face his congregation of one and intones the Dismissal and the final Blessing.

To his surprise, George hasn't left. Instead he comes up to the altar and says, 'Let me give you a hand putting everything away.'

And he does.

'Thank you,' says John Elliott, when they have finished.

'No, thank you,' says George. 'After all, it isn't often one has one's own personal church service.'

'It was very good of you to brave the elements,' says John Elliott. He's not sure that George isn't having fun at his expense: there's a sardonic quality to his speech that is unsettling.

Then George says, 'You may not see me here for a while. That's why I made a special effort to come in today.'

'Oh? Are you going away?'

'Perhaps for a while,' says George. 'Who knows? Perhaps for ever.' He doesn't offer to shake the vicar's hand. He gives a short wave and then leaves, stepping into the icy cold outside.

As John Elliott locks up the church, he ponders George's last remark. It doesn't sound like the sort of thing a well-balanced person would say. But then, he's always known George was odd. Then he reproaches himself: isn't that what the Church is for, to offer comfort to those who are sick in mind as well as body? Isn't George exactly the sort of person a conscientious vicar would reach out to? He goes home, feeling rather ridiculous when he has to report to Christine that he gave a service for a congregation of one.

Over lunch she says, 'I wonder if we'll be open at the school tomorrow. Quite a lot of the children won't be able to get there if this snow gets any worse.'

'Well, if you need a volunteer to dig out paths, let me know,' says John. A bit of physical exercise might be just what he needs.

'Oh, thank you, sweetheart,' says Christine. 'I might very well do that if we don't get a thaw.'

They don't get a thaw. That afternoon the sky darkens early and heavy flakes of snow begin to drift down again. The vicar stares out of the window at them: they are like an invasion from an alien world, transforming his own, making it unrecognisable to him. Even with the central heating turned up, a rare luxury, the little house feels cold.

They go to bed early that evening, huddling together under the duvet to find some warmth. It's a long time before John Elliott drifts off to sleep, and even then a restless unease seems to invade his dreams. He dreams of nothing and everything: he's in church again and George's snout-like face is giving its sideways smile at him, a smile that is empty of all meaning. He hears a voice ask: 'What if it's all true?' At first he thinks it is George who must have spoken, but then he remembers it was somebody else who said those words to him. In his dream, he can't remember who it was.

A moment ago, he was in his church. Now he's outside it, in the churchyard, without knowing how he got there. It is still snowing and, at the same time, he can see stars in the sky, stars everywhere in the gaps between ragged black clouds. Their radiance is ten times the normal, a hundred times. He hears a woman gasp, somewhere nearby. It's not a gasp of pain. Then the stars are hidden and it seems to John Elliott that giant black wings have unfolded, cutting out the light. He shouts out in fear and wakes himself up.

'Oh, now what's the matter?' asks Christine, switching on her bedside lamp.

'I had a bad dream,' says John Elliott, sitting bolt upright and looking around the bedroom in confusion. In his mind he can still hear the beating of enormous wings. Christine is about to say something cross, but then catches sight of her husband's face.

'Come and cuddle up with me,' she says instead.

They cuddle up.

The next morning, they wake to a sky of the palest blue. It's stopped snowing, but there are another couple of inches lying on top of the foot that was already there. Once they've dressed and are drinking their mugs of tea in the kitchen, Christine rings up the headmistress, whose grace-and-favour house abuts the grounds of the school, to ask if they're going to open today.

'Yes, we'll do our best, but we need to dig out the snow between the road and the school buildings, and across the playground too.'

John Elliott is reminded of his offer to help, and agrees gladly. It's beautiful outside, and the exercise will do him the world of good. There's no question of driving to the school. Snowploughs are out clearing and gritting the main roads, but it will be a while before they reach this part of town. They walk arm in arm to the school, and every now and then one of them slips or staggers on a patch of ice and is steadied by the other. This feeling of mutual dependency brings them closer. This is how they used to be, thinks John Elliott. When did it ever stop? If I can't keep loving my own wife, he tells himself, what chance have I of sustaining an abstract love for an abstract God? Then he reproaches himself. God is not abstract, but real and present. That is what he believes; what he wants to believe.

They arrive at the school. By the gates, Billy, the school's maintenance man, is handing out plastic snow shovels.

'I went down Friday night and got the last ones in Tesco's,' he tells them proudly. Three staff members and a couple of strong-looking men who must be parents are already shovelling a path from the gates towards the entrance to the school. John and Christine Elliott join in and soon a path has been opened up as far as the main building. Children and their parents are starting to arrive and it's likely that some form of schooling will take place today. Christine goes inside and John Elliott and a couple of other men head across to the playground to start clearing that.

As the vicar bends to lift a shovelful of snow, a snowball hits him on the back. He turns to see that a small group of children have slipped away from the main building and have started to play in the snow. He's not sure whether

156

the snowball was aimed at him. It seems more likely that it was an overthrow from a battle that has begun nearby. He's been caught in the crossfire.

At that moment one of the children turns away from the others, laughing, and runs to get out of range of a couple of other boys who are trying to land a snowball on him. Then he slips and falls, hands stretched outwards to save himself. He falls into a pile of shovelled snow. It seems unlikely that he is hurt but, all the same, John Elliott, as the nearest adult, hurries across the playground to make sure he's all right. The child – a small boy – is struggling to his feet and John Elliott helps him. As he bends over the boy, he notices two things. The first is that the boy is the child called Theo whom he met here a few days ago. The second is that where Theo put his hands out to save himself as he fell into the snow bank, the snow is pink and red with blood.

'Theo! Are you hurt?' asks John Elliott. He grabs both the boy's hands and turns them palm up. In the centre of each palm is a hole the size of a twenty-pence piece. The inside of the hole is dark and crusted and bloody. The outside edges are purple with bruising and scratch marks and more blood. Why Theo isn't screaming in agony isn't immediately obvious. Instead, he's smiling at John Elliott. He doesn't seem to be aware that anything is wrong.

'Who did this to you?' asks John Elliott in a fury. Then, collecting himself, he asks: 'Does it hurt much?'

'It doesn't hurt at all,' replies Theo. 'I only slipped.'

Then a curious thing happens. As John Elliott looks at the wounds on Theo's hands, they appear to fade. One moment it looks as if Theo is going to be heading for the nearest A&E if ever an ambulance can get up the hill. The next, it's just as if he's been gripping some sharp object too tightly in both hands. And the next moment, both palms appear pink and healthy. John Elliott lets go of Theo's hands and looks for the bloodstains in the snow. But someone has shovelled fresh snow and rock salt onto the pile where Theo fell and the stains are either hidden, or gone.

Five

'I didn't imagine it,' says John Elliott in exasperation.

'You must have done,' says Christine. They are sitting at the kitchen table having supper, and the conversation has been going round in circles for some time. 'I mean, what are the alternatives? That Mary and What's-his-name have been torturing the child and then sent him to school? And why weren't the marks there when I looked at Theo? It can only have been five minutes later when I came out into the playground.'

'I don't know,' replies John Elliott in a grim voice. 'What does that make me, then? Mad?'

'You don't have to be mad to see things that aren't there,' Christine tells him. 'If you're tired, or overstrained, the mind can play tricks on you. Sometimes people see things just because they want to see them.'

'Or don't want to see them,' says her husband. 'Anyway, why would I want to see poor Theo with holes in his hands?'

There's a long, long pause. John Elliott gets up from the table, puts the kettle on, then comes back and sits down again. Christine hasn't answered his question.

'So what's the answer?' repeats John Elliott. 'Why would I?'

Very softly, she replies at last. 'Maybe it had some religious significance for you?'

'Religious significance? What on earth can you mean? Oh—'

Then he remembers a verse from the text he was reading from in church a couple of weeks ago: the Epistle of St Paul to the Galatians. 'I bear on my body the marks of Jesus.'

'Oh, come on, Christine,' he says. When John Elliott gets excited or angry, his speech tends to regress from the slightest inflection of a Scottish accent to the dialect of his childhood: the rich Borders speech of the men and women who lived in the valleys of the Oxnam Water, Jed Water and the Teviot, that all flow into the great Tweed. 'I'm no' daft, ye ken? I'm no' some idiot.'

Christine puts her hand on his arm.

'Don't be upset, John,' she urges him. 'It's just that you've been putting yourself under a lot of pressure these last few months. It's a thankless job you've taken on at St Joseph's. Sometimes I think you'd have a bigger congregation if you were ministering to a church in – I don't know – the middle of Libya or somewhere.'

Her husband can't help laughing at the thought. The tension goes out of his face. When he next speaks, his speech is normal. 'It's not easy,' he says. 'I'll admit that. It's very far from easy.'

This time, Christine gets up as the kettle comes to the boil. She makes them Nescafé and brings the mugs back to the table. She doesn't want the conversation to end just yet.

'You know, you're still young, John. You don't have to stay in this job if it doesn't work out. There's no point in grinding yourself down, the way you have been, if it's maybe never going to come out right. We've only the one life.'

'And what do you think we'd do if I gave up this job – and this house? Sleep on the streets?'

Christine hesitates because she's been thinking about what she's going to say next for some months, and she doesn't want it to come out the wrong way.

'You know, if we moved back to the Borders, to Kelso, there are plenty of folk my parents know who'd be happy to take you on. You're known as a hard worker, and people would find you a job for your father's sake, or mine. And I could find teaching work. I've still got friends in the profession up there and we're both Scots – we'd find work.'

'It's all moonshine,' says John Elliott. 'I'm not going to run away from this place with my tail between my legs. I'm going to go and watch television.'

Christine hasn't achieved much so far, but she is happier. She knows her man. He won't forget what she's said. She's planted a seed of doubt in his mind. There's no doubt at all in hers. She's decided her husband is a square peg in a round hole, and she's going to do what she can to save him.

Over the next few days, this new idea takes root in John Elliott's mind, and begins to send tendrils of thought into his consciousness that might not have come to him in any other way. A few days later, at breakfast, he announces to Christine: 'I'm going to pop down to Durham at lunchtime. They want me to meet some of the new student intake and chat to them about life on the outside. I'll only be there a couple of hours. Can you manage without the car today?'

His voice is offhand, as if what he has just said is not of the least importance. Christine doesn't believe a word of it. She has a fair idea why her husband might be going back to his old university, but all she says is, 'Oh, well, try not to put them off too much. I don't need the car.'

She guesses that he is going to see Dr Blair, his former tutor and, inwardly, she's jubilant. She thinks: he's going to ask his tutor's advice about his job and the doubts he's been having. He really has been thinking about what I've said.

In the late morning, John Elliott drives down to Durham. The roads are clear now, and the snow has retreated to piles of frozen slush along the verges. The fields are still white, and it remains very cold. The sky is a leaden grey. By midday, he's parked in the city, as near as he can get to the cathedral. He has arranged to meet Dr Blair in a nearby pub. Talking to him in his room in college would be too much like being back in a tutorial. He needs to be on neutral ground. And he knows Dr Blair is fond of a pint of beer.

'So, how are you keeping, John?' asks Dr Blair, taking a long sip of his pint and then wiping the foam from his upper lip. Dr Blair is a small, wiry man dressed in a tweed jacket and yellow corduroy trousers. His black hair has more grey in it than John Elliott remembers, but it is still plentiful, sitting in tight curls on Dr Blair's head and slightly longer than you would expect from a man in his fifties. His face, too, is more lined and his brown eyes have sunk deeper but, in every other way, Dr Blair is unchanged: energetic in manner, decisive in speech and deep in thought.

'I'm fine, thank you,' says John Elliott.

'Fine? Well, that sounds good. And how is the lovely Christine?'

Dr Blair was a guest at the Elliotts' wedding just over two years ago.

'She's fine too.'

'And our church? Is that fine as well?'

'It's a work in progress. We had some vandals strip lead from the roof the other day.'

Dr Blair makes appropriate noises of anger and disgust and then they talk about things in general at St Joseph's, and in a few minutes Dr Blair has a picture of John Elliott's life and his struggles with his congregation. It's not so much what John Elliott tells him; it's what he doesn't tell him. It's time for another pint. Dr Blair gets them in, and as he sits back down at the table he says, 'Well, are you enjoying it all?'

'Enjoying it?'

'You were lucky to get a parish when you did, you know. I imagine you want to make the most of the opportunity. Not every young priest has been as fortunate as you have.'

John Elliott seems to be about to say something, but he doesn't speak, and he doesn't touch the fresh pint in front of him. Dr Blair raises one eyebrow, in the way he used to do in tutorials, and then his former pupil finds his voice. 'No, to tell you the truth, I'm not enjoying it.'

'You're not?'

'It sounds ungrateful, I know. But sometimes I wonder whether I'm the right man for the job.'

Then it all comes out: the unsuccessful struggle to increase the congregation; the impossibility of ever meeting the financial targets set for the Parish Share; the sullen indifference to the church on the part of most of his parishioners. Dr Blair listens patiently, an expression of sympathy on his face, until John Elliott winds down. Then he frowns suddenly and says, 'Did you think it was going to be easy?'

'No.'

'Then why all the whingeing?'

John Elliott stares at his old tutor in shock. He'd been expecting sympathy, a friendly hand patting him on the back.

'I'm not . . .' he begins, but Dr Blair interrupts him.

'You signed on to do a job. You've only been at it for two years and now you're looking for an excuse to give up. Get a grip, John. This is real life, not a game show. Do the job you accepted with open hands and stop complaining.'

John Elliott is a proud man and he doesn't like being told off. He pushes his full pint away from him and starts to stand up, but his tutor reaches out and puts a hand on his shoulder, gently pushing him back down into his chair.

'Don't tell me you can't take a bit of straight talking,' says Dr Blair.

'You're right, of course . . .' says John Elliott in a moody voice. 'If only that was all.'

'What do you mean?'

Then John Elliott tells him about Theo. He tells him about the football game where he first met Theo, and then he tells him about their second encounter: Theo running across the snow-covered playground and slipping and falling. He tells Dr Blair about the blood in the snow. He describes the marks he saw on the palms of Theo's hands and how they faded, then vanished. He doesn't know what sort of reaction he's expecting to this story. In truth, he doesn't understand his own feelings on the subject. But he doesn't expect the response he gets.

'Child abuse,' says Dr Blair, in a horrified voice. 'It sounds like violence of the worst sort. Poor little boy. Have you reported it to the police?'

'Well, no. Report what? The marks disappeared. I told you that.'

'You mean, they were never there in the first place?'

'Yes, they were there. Just as you're here now, sitting in front of me.'

Dr Blair takes another long drink from his pint. Then he says, 'I'm sorry, I don't understand. You saw wounds in the palms of his hands one minute and the next minute they weren't there?'

'Exactly.'

Dr Blair thinks for a moment. 'You're not making much sense. The marks probably weren't there in the first place. It doesn't change my advice, though. If there's even a remote possibility that the boy has been harmed, you must report it to the police or at least to the school.'

John Elliott doesn't answer straight away. Then he asks, 'Could there be another explanation, do you think?'

'You tell me,' suggests Dr Blair. 'You were there.'

'It occurred to me,' says John Elliott in a diffident voice, 'that it could have been stigmata.'

There's a long pause. When Dr Blair speaks again, John Elliott can hear genuine anger in his voice.

'Stigmata? *Stigmata*? Leave that sort of nonsense to the Church of Rome,' says Dr Blair. 'You need to get your head back on straight, Elliott.' No first names now. 'Either you saw the marks, in which case you should report them. Or else you didn't. If there's any doubt at all in your mind, you should go to the school or the police. But for heaven's sake, don't just sit on it. And once you've passed on the information, don't get involved any further. If the press find out you've known about a potential case of child abuse and that you've concealed it from the authorities, for whatever reason, your name and the good name of the church will be dragged through the mud.'

Dr Blair drains the remaining beer in his glass. Then he stands up and looks at his watch. 'I must go. I've a tutorial in half an hour. Come and see me again in a few months. I hope next time we meet, I will find you more like the positive young man I remember from our tutorials.'

John Elliott mumbles goodbye and sits looking at his untouched pint. He doesn't want to have any more to drink. After a few moments, he stands up, leaves the pub and walks up the narrow street that leads to the cathedral. Durham Cathedral and Durham Castle sit upon a mound above the town and the river. He'd lived within sight of this building for three years not that long ago, but it still awes him whenever he revisits it, as if he were seeing it for the first time. He enters the nave and walks up between the tall columns of stone and gazes at the rib vaults above. At last he comes to the Neville Screen, behind which is the Chapel of the Nine Altars. He remembers the story of how, during the Dissolution of the Monasteries, commissioners of King Henry VIII were instructed to open the tomb of Saint Cuthbert and cast out the bones of the saint. But when they opened the tomb, they found the body of the saint 'whole and uncorrupted' after lying there for 900 years. The commissioners closed up the tomb, but in the end it was broken open again on the king's orders, and the saint's remains were mingled with those of others and buried below the chapel.

Was that another miracle? People thought so at the time, but John Elliott knows that the body had been embalmed and mummified. It wasn't a miracle, just a little piece of technology that had been forgotten for a while. There was always a rational explanation for these things. People saw

166

what they wanted to see; sometimes people saw what they didn't want to see. They didn't always see what was there.

That was the case with Theo, he decides. His eyes had tricked him. His senses had tricked him. It had seemed so very real at the time, but of course it had been some kind of illusion, a mental trick played on him by his tired brain.

John Elliott leaves the cathedral in a better frame of mind. The place has worked its magic on him once more. He finds his car and drives home.

Six

He arrives home at about half past three and, as he opens the door, the first thing he hears is the sound of the phone ringing. It stops as he enters the hall and then starts again a moment later. He picks up in the kitchen. It's Christine.

'Oh, John, thank God. I've been trying to get you for ages. Why don't you ever have your mobile with you?'

John has, once again, left it on the kitchen table.

'I'm sorry, I forgot it. What's the emergency?'

'Can you come to the school? Right away? As quickly as you can?'

Christine hangs up before he can ask any more questions. He can't imagine what the problem is, but he can hear the urgency in her voice. He hurries back to the car and drives to the school. He parks as close to the gates as he can – parents are already arriving to collect their children – and walks in through the main entrance. He's not sure where to find Christine, but then he recognises a member of staff who tells him she's in the gym block. He leaves the main building and jogs across the playground, now free of snow apart from a frozen mound in one corner. He finds the gym empty, but he can hear voices coming from the changing rooms.

He heads across to the door and sees Christine, the

headmistress and two men he does not recognise. A fifth person is lying on a bench, his eyes closed. It's Theo; John Elliott recognises him instantly. He's removed his shirt and pullover for some reason and has a towel draped over the top half of his body. Without opening his eyes, the boy says sleepily, 'Hello, Mr Elliott. I'm glad you've come.'

John Elliott asks Christine, and the room in general, 'What's going on? Why am I here?'

Christine defers to the headmistress, who says, 'Your wife says you've seen something like this before. I am amazed you didn't get in touch with me at the time, but we can talk about that later. These two gentlemen are Dr Carter, the GP who looks after the school when needed, and this is Mr Griffith Jones, who is a Domestic Violence Prevention Officer from the council.'

Dr Carter, a tall man in a tweed suit, is holding a small camera. 'I've taken some photographs,' he says. 'We have the evidence. But the marks seem to be fading. Come and look, vicar, and tell us if this is what you told your wife you saw last week.'

He bids John Elliott to cross the room and examine Theo. Bending over Theo, he's conscious of how calm the boy is: his handsome face is so relaxed he looks as if he's almost asleep. His eyes are still shut. John Elliott picks up the boy's hands and examines each palm in turn. There is a circular blue bruise with an angry red centre in the middle of each one. The doctor removes the towel to reveal a red weal below the boy's ribs on his left side, as if someone has struck him with a stick or perhaps a whip.

'His feet, too,' says Dr Carter. The marks on the palms are replicated on the feet below the tarsal joint. 'Is this what you saw?'

'Does it hurt, Theo?' asks John Elliott.

'No. Can I go soon?'

Theo opens his eyes and looks directly into the eyes of John Elliott, who feels a sense of shock, as if a window has been opened somewhere and a cold draught has swept into the room. He straightens up and says, 'I saw something like this before, but only on the palms of his hands.'

'You didn't think of mentioning this?' asks Dr Carter incredulously. 'You didn't consider this might be abuse?'

'The marks faded almost straight away. These are fading too. Look.'

Dr Carter, the small man who was introduced as Griffith Jones, and the headmistress all come forward and bend over the boy. The purple weal is still visible below his ribs, but now looks nothing more than a scratch. The marks on his palms and feet are like faint bruises, as if the boy might have knocked himself playing football. The angry red at the centre of each mark has disappeared.

'Well, I don't know what to say,' says Dr Carter. 'He's making a remarkable recovery.'

'It doesn't change anything,' says Griffith Jones. 'You have the photographs. This child has clearly been subjected to violence.'

'Not here,' says the headmistress sharply.

Before the conversation can go any further, Theo sits up and says, 'My mother is at the gate now. She's worried because I haven't come out from school yet.'

Somehow nobody doubts this statement. In a moment, Theo is dressed in his shirt and grey pullover and is walking with Christine to go and meet his mother.

'Ask Mrs Constantine to join us in my study,' the headmistress instructs Christine as she sets off towards the

170

school gates. 'The rest of you, please accompany me there now.'

The headmistress's study is an austere room, with a large desk, some filing cabinets and framed school photographs on the wall. The headmistress sits behind the desk and steeples her hands. She doesn't invite anyone else to sit down. She addresses Griffith Jones first. 'What steps do you propose to take, Mr Jones?'

Griffith Jones says, 'Well, it's a little early to be definitive about this, but . . .' And he begins to talk about risk assessments, violence prevention and perpetrator-management programmes. He is interrupted by the return of Christine. She is alone.

'Where is Mrs Constantine?' asks the headmistress.

'She said she hadn't time to see you this afternoon, she had shopping to do.'

'Really,' says the headmistress. She appears quite shocked at this affront to her authority. If she requires a parent's presence in her study, she is accustomed to that parent attending to her wishes. 'You should have insisted, Christine.'

'Well, I couldn't, really,' says Christine. 'Theo seemed perfectly happy and all the marks we saw had disappeared. What could I say?'

John Elliott glances at Christine. He doesn't say, 'I told you so', but his look says it for him. Christine gives an unhappy little shrug of her shoulders. Meanwhile, the headmistress is asking the doctor what could have produced the marks on Theo, if not physical violence.

'The marks could have been some kind of haemorrhagic lesion,' says Dr Carter. 'But he had no fever. His temperature was on the low side, if anything.'

'Can you translate that into English?' asks the headmistress.

'Well, you get lesions with some strains of meningitis, for example,' suggests the doctor.

'There's no meningitis in *my* school,' says the headmistress angrily. She is silent for a few minutes, thinking, and nobody wants to interrupt her train of thought. After a moment she says, 'I am inclined not to report this to the police at present. We have very little evidence that any harm has been done to Theo, and no firm evidence as to when and how it happened. I don't want any unnecessary scandal, so I would appreciate it if you could all keep the matter confidential for the moment.'

There's a murmur of agreement from John and Christine Elliott and Dr Carter. Griffith Jones looks disappointed. The headmistress continues.

'However, if anything like this happens again to Theo Constantine, I will definitely involve the police and you, too, Mr Jones. Dr Carter, I would be grateful for copies of the photographs you have taken as soon as they are available.'

'I'll email them to you tonight,' says Dr Carter.

Christine and John Elliott leave the school together. At the gates, Griffith Jones catches up with them. He is a small, plump man, and has put on a bright-blue down jacket with the hood up, a garment of the sort worn by polar explorers.

'Now then, vicar,' he says, blowing on his gloved hands and rubbing them. 'It's cold enough, isn't it?'

The steeple tower of St Joseph's is silhouetted against a darkening red sky. The temperature has dropped to well below freezing.

172

'What can I do for you?' asks John Elliott. His voice is as chilly as the weather: he does not like Griffith Jones.

'Do I gather that you've seen these marks on Theo before? Can you tell me about that?'

John Elliott doesn't want to tell this man anything, but he does not see how he can refuse. He tells the story of Theo in the playground as briefly as he can without being downright rude. Then he and Christine start to walk away.

'Mind if I walk with you for a bit?' asks Griffith Jones. They can't stop him. The vicar nods curtly and the three of them set off down the hill.

'Must be marvellous being a vicar,' says Griffith Jones. 'Dealing with people is what it's all about, isn't that right, vicar?'

'It's part of it,' the vicar agrees.

'That's what I do too. Domestic Violence Prevention Officer. That's my title. It's a lovely job. I meet some lovely people, even if some of them are a bit dysfunctional.'

Not receiving any reply from either of the Elliotts, Griffith Jones takes this as permission to keep talking. 'Now that child, Theo. In my experience, there's no smoke without fire. Those marks on his body are the result of physical violence. The doctor won't say so, but I do say so.'

'Really?' says the vicar.

'Indeed. Maybe they were hysterical in origin, but that boy's been traumatised and I'm betting it was the parents. It nearly always is.'

By now, the three of them have come to the pedestrian lane that runs up towards St Joseph's Church, and then down the other side to the small housing estate where the Elliotts live.

'This is the parting of the ways,' says the vicar.

173

'Ah, the parting of the ways,' says Griffith Jones in delight, as if the vicar has just made a tremendously witty remark. 'You take the high road and I'll take the low road, and I'll get to Scotland afore ye. Yes, Theo Constantine is a candidate for an Emergency Protection Order. I shouldn't be surprised if he were in council care by Christmas. Keep me posted, Mr and Mrs Elliott, if you see any more injuries on that child. I'm counting on you.'

Seven

It is often the case that once normality has been interrupted in someone's life, it is difficult to restore the balance. Once it has gone, one looks back to the tedium of daily life before as a golden time of peace and happiness, regardless of how dull it might once have seemed. All the certainties, once so achingly predictable, disappear and one longs for their return.

John Elliott would give almost anything to go back to those days when all he had to think about were the daily routines of his parish.

Now he is troubled. He is troubled about the meaning of his job. He feels futile and ineffective. He wonders whether this is attributable to the circumstances of this particular parish. He suspects, however, that it is a fundamental defect in his own qualities as a parish priest.

He is troubled by his encounters with Theo. He cannot think of any explanation for the appearance and disappearance of the injuries he has seen on the child. Nor can he understand why he has been chosen – that is how it feels to him – as a witness. He cannot really believe that he is witnessing stigmata: the idea offends his sense of the rational. To someone brought up in the Church of Scotland and now ordained in the Church of England, the intrusion of the miraculous seems almost like bad taste. Only God or his Son can perform miracles, and there are many who are reluctant to admit even as much as that.

But then, what is the explanation for what he has seen? The doctor's speculations seem to him no more than medical quackery. And, if the marks were the result of a physical assault on the child, he cannot understand when and where and how that assault took place.

Christine is also subdued by what she has seen. She is inclined to favour the theory that child abuse has occurred, but she is honest enough to be puzzled as to how the marks on Theo's body have appeared and then disappeared so quickly. They don't like to talk about it much; the whole situation is unsatisfactory logically, and (in John Elliott's view) theologically.

But, of course, they do talk about it a little. As they eat their supper in the little kitchen that evening, Christine says, 'What gets me is that, of all the mothers I've seen, Mary Constantine seems the least likely to harm her own child. Some of them . . . Well, some of the mothers have to be seen to be believed. You wouldn't be at all surprised to hear they'd just got out of prison. But not Mary.'

'I think you said you've never met her partner. He's the stepfather, isn't he?'

'Geordie Nixon? No, I haven't met him. And maybe he's the one who's been harming Theo, although I still can't quite see when and how. I'd like to meet him. Perhaps he'll be at the school for the Christmas play.'

They settle down in front of the television to watch the ten o'clock news. At least, John Elliott watches it, while Christine marks some homework. At a quarter past ten, the phone rings, and John Elliott looks at his wife with a raised eyebrow. Who on earth could be calling them at this time of night? He almost decides not to answer it, but then it occurs to him that it might be one of his parishioners. He picks up the phone.

'Hello? Is that the Reverend John Elliott?' asks a woman's voice.

'Yes, who is this?'

'Dr Mindrum. I'm the registrar at St Mark's. I believe you know one of our patients, Alfred Stone?'

With some apprehension, John Elliott admits they've met. He adds, 'But I can't really say that I know him.'

'He seems very familiar with you. He speaks of you as an old friend. Anyway, the reason I'm calling is to tell you that we are very worried about him. His condition has deteriorated badly in the last few days and he's lost a lot of weight. He's very unsettled. This morning he started asking for you, he wants you to come and see him. He won't stop. He's just wearing himself out.'

'Come and see him?' repeats John Elliott in a dull voice, knowing what must come next.

'Yes, come and see him. We really don't know if he'll last the night. We've tried mild sedation, but it's made no difference. He insists that he has to see you as soon as possible.'

'But it's half past ten at night,' John Elliott says. He is disgusted by the whining sound of his own voice.

'I know it's late, but he says he must see you. It's up to you, of course. But I'm afraid that if you leave it until tomorrow, it may be too late. We're very anxious to calm him down and your presence at his bedside might help. Nothing else we've been able to try has worked.'

John Elliott puts his hand over the mouthpiece and explains the situation to Christine. She is surprised, but then says, 'I suppose you'd better go. There's no special reason for you to be up first thing tomorrow morning, is there? Take your keys with you, I'll be in bed before you get back.'

With great reluctance, John Elliott levers himself out of his armchair. His body seems to weigh twice what it did earlier in the day, but he manages to put on his cap and coat and gloves. He calls to Christine that he'll see her later, and receives a distracted reply: she is still deep in the task of marking homework. Then he opens the front door to see a full moon riding high in the sky between ragged clouds. The cold makes him shudder even with all his winter clothes on.

At that time of night, the roads are empty, but here and there he sees the dull sheen of black ice, so he drives with great care. Even so, it doesn't take him long to get to St Mark's. He's there far too soon. He's not looking forward to his second interview with Alfred Stone. At Reception he asks for Dr Mindrum and, in a few minutes, a dark-haired woman in her forties appears. She greets him with a brisk handshake.

'I'm so grateful you've come, vicar,' she tells him. 'It may not do any good, but we felt we had to ask. Poor Alfred seems so desperate to see you.'

The building is deserted. Only the night lights are on in the corridors, making them seem longer and gloomier than John Elliott remembers. From behind closed doors he hears mutterings and coughing, and once he hears a loud scream from further up the corridor. Dr Mindrum hears it too. She pauses for a second and then says, 'I'll just look in on Alfred and make sure everything is all right. Then I'd better go and see what that noise was about.'

She knocks lightly on the next door they come to, and unlocks it. The room is in darkness, but in the light from the corridor John Elliott sees a man twisting and turning on the bed. Most of the bedclothes are on the floor.

'Alfred, the Reverend Elliott has come all this way to see you.' She propels John Elliott further into the room with a hand on his back and adds, 'I'll send a nurse along in a moment to tuck you up in bed. What a tangle you've got your sheets in. Now I'm going to switch on the light so that the poor vicar doesn't have to sit here in the dark.'

Then she's gone, and John Elliott is alone with Alfred Stone. He sees a solitary chair pushed against the wall and drags it across so he can sit at the bedside. Before he can speak, Alfred Stone sits up. In the glare of the overhead light he looks like an awakened corpse. The pallor of his skin and the emaciation of his features suggest approaching dissolution. John Elliott is shocked by the change in the man's appearance since his last visit. Before he can greet him, Alfred says, 'My dear boy, it is so kind of you to come and visit me at such a late hour. A truly generous act, for which I am very grateful.'

'I was told you'd been asking for me.'

'Indeed I have. I'm sorry I can't offer you any refreshment after your journey. A little glass of sherry might have been welcome. I think it must be cold outside. They keep this place so overheated it is hard for me to tell, and the window is locked in case I try to escape. Imagine! I find it hard enough to take a shower on my own, let alone go climbing out of windows. But it's procedure, they tell me.'

'It's very cold tonight,' agrees John Elliott, not knowing what else to say.

'And have you been having the dreams?'

179

'I'm not sure what you mean,' replies the vicar, but even as he does so the memory of a dream floods into his mind: an angel with black wings beating in the snow, above the graveyard of St Joseph's. He realises he has had this dream not once, but several times. His conscious mind had suppressed the memory, but Alfred Stone's question has brought it back.

'Ah, I see that you have.'

He doesn't know whether to deny any such thing. He has an awful feeling this man is reading his mind.

'Do you want to know what I saw at St Joseph's that night?'

Before John Elliott can say no, he doesn't want to hear any more of this madness, Alfred Stone continues, 'I went up to the churchyard one night. I don't know what made me go there at such an odd time of day. It was like a tickling feeling – an itch in my mind. Anyway, I had to go.'

John Elliott sits up straighter in his chair and stares at Alfred Stone, who laughs quietly.

'I see I'm ringing some bells here,' he says pleasantly. For a moment, the vicar finds it impossible to believe this man is mad after all; his manner is so relaxed and conversational.

'Go on,' he says.

'When I reached the churchyard, at first it was very quiet. It was dark, of course, but not so dark that I couldn't see at all. I could make out the shapes of the gravestones. Then I heard a noise.'

'A noise? What kind of noise?'

'I heard a gasp. It sounded like a woman's voice. I turned towards the sound and what do you think I saw then?'

John Elliott finds that he is gripping the sides of his chair so tightly that his knuckles have gone white. Alfred Stone waits for a moment, then says, 'I saw someone lying on a grave marker. I think it was a woman, although it was hard to make out any detail in the darkness. I suppose I thought that because of the sound I'd heard earlier. I decided to approach her, to see whether she needed help.'

Alfred Stone gives John Elliott a pleading look. For the moment he seems utterly sane. He asks, 'You do believe me, don't you?'

'Go on,' repeats John Elliott.

'Then I saw another figure. It was dark so I couldn't see properly. But it seemed to be taller than any man should be. The figure was bent over the woman lying on the grave. I wondered if she would scream, but she didn't. Then I couldn't see any more.'

'Why not? What happened?'

'Because the tall figure unfolded its wings. They were enormous, and black, and they beat once or twice with a clapping noise. I couldn't see the woman any more. She was covered by the wings.'

'What did you do?' asks the vicar.

'What did I do? What would you have done, I wonder? I ran. I ran home and locked the door. I knelt and prayed that I had not gone mad.'

John Elliott can't speak. This is so like his dreams. Has this poor, mentally unbalanced man somehow read his mind? Except, just at the moment, despite the story he has told, he doesn't sound deranged. Then Alfred Stone says, 'I don't know what you make of all that.'

'What do you make of it?'

Instead of answering, Alfred Stone remarks, 'It was thinking too much about the events of that night that resulted in my ending up in this place.'

181

'I'm sorry you should have been burdened like that.'

'Burdened? I was chosen. As you have been. And have you met him yet?'

'Have I met who?'

Alfred Stone gives a knowing smile. The effect is ghastly on his skull-like face, the skin stretched taut over the protruding cheekbones, large, yellow teeth exposed by his drawn-back lips.

'Perhaps you haven't recognised him yet. He would be about nine or ten years old. It was ten years ago I witnessed that event in the churchyard at St Joseph's. I tried to suppress the memories for many years, but then they just became too much . . .'

John Elliott remains silent. He doesn't know what to say to all this. Alfred Stone is insane, after all. There is no means of communicating with him in a rational manner.

Then Alfred Stone reaches out a bony hand, startling John Elliott, and grabs the lapel of his overcoat, pulling him closer to the bed.

'He's in great danger. You must save him. He has only weeks, perhaps days, to live if someone doesn't help him. You must protect him. You must watch over him day and night.'

'I'm not sure who you are talking about,' says the vicar. But this is ingenuous. He is beginning to have an awful idea that this madman is talking about Theo. But how does he know of Theo's existence? And why does he talk about him in this particular way?

'Do you deny him? If only I were stronger, I would leave this place and rescue him myself.'

At that moment, Dr Mindrum returns with a nurse entering the room behind her. The conversation is interrupted. John Elliott stands up so that Alfred Stone can struggle into the chair while the nurse makes up the bed for him with fresh sheets. Then Alfred Stone starts to murmur. At first his words are too faint to understand, but then his voice becomes louder. It rings around the room. 'He comes amongst us unrecognised. He has tried to return to us many times over the centuries. Each time they murder him.'

Dr Mindrum says: 'Alfred, please keep your voice down. You'll wake the other patients.'

'I'm afraid I'm not doing any good here,' suggests John Elliott. He is desperate to get away from this hot room, from the ramblings of this poor, mad, former priest.

'He's becoming very anxious again. I'll have to give him another injection,' says Dr Mindrum. She hurries from the room. The nurse tells Alfred to get back into bed, and helps him climb between the newly made sheets. The old man does what she wants obediently, but then sits up and shouts: 'He won't like being sacrificed again, you know.'

'There, there,' says the nurse. 'Try and speak a little more quietly.'

Alfred turns his attention again to John Elliott and repeats, 'You must save him. That's why you have been chosen.'

'You ought to get some sleep,' answers John Elliott.

At that moment, Dr Mindrum returns with a syringe, and the nurse rolls up the pyjama sleeve on Alfred Stone's left arm. Dr Mindrum injects the syringe into the vein in the crook of the arm and, a moment later, Alfred Stone lays his head back on his pillow. He looks close to death. He murmurs something that John Elliott cannot make out, then his eyes close and he is asleep, or unconscious.

183

'I don't think I did any good,' the vicar tells Dr Mindrum.

'We had to try. Thank you for coming anyway.'

'I'll call in the morning to see how he is.'

'Yes. Do that,' replies the doctor. 'Let's hope he can get some rest now. He's very weak.'

There seems little else to say. If the intention was to help Alfred Stone, John Elliott's journey has been futile. His presence seems to have excited him to the limits of his failing strength.

Or perhaps the journey wasn't pointless, as far as Alfred Stone is concerned. He had something to tell John Elliott and he's told him.

John Elliott drives home through flurries of snow that now speckle the black roads. The full moon is lower in the sky when he arrives home, but the light is still strong enough to cast a faint shadow. Outside his house he sees the spire of St Joseph's towering above him, a couple of hundred yards up the hill. He wonders what he might find in the churchyard if he went there and, for a moment, he almost considers heading in that direction. Then he shakes his head and walks up the path to his house. There is just enough snow to leave faint outlines of his footprints. He unlocks the front door as quietly as he can and goes to the cupboard above the kitchen sink where a whisky bottle sits. It is there for guests. He rarely touches the stuff, but tonight is an exception. He pours a generous slug into a glass and drains it in a couple of gulps.

Eight

There's to be a drinks party at the Elliotts' house the next evening. The parish newsletter announced that it is to be held at 'the vicarage'. Vicarage may be the correct term for a vicar's house, but in no other way does their house resemble the large Victorian stone-built manse that once stood on the site of the housing estate where the Elliotts now live. Nor will it be easy to squeeze many guests into the small kitchen and living room, although they have to try.

It takes John Elliott a while to surface after his troubled night. Once he is awake, he goes downstairs to find a note in the kitchen reminding him to buy the wine and food for the evening's entertainment. In his efforts to wake up and get himself organised, John Elliott forgets all about St Mark's for the moment. He forgets all about Alfred Stone.

He does the shopping and tidies the house, and the day passes quickly. Christine arrives home from school at five and there is just an hour left before the first guests will arrive, giving the Elliotts barely enough time to set out the hired wine glasses and the saucers of pickled onions and cubes of cheese with cocktail sticks stuck through them. Christine goes upstairs to change while her husband braces himself for the first arrivals.

The vicar finds these evenings torture, but they are a good way to raise money for the church. Tickets cost five pounds each and, in addition, there is a raffle. The local cinema has donated two tickets for its next show. A bottle of Bulgarian red wine is the second prize and there are various other modest gifts, mostly boxes of chocolates or packets of biscuits.

At one minute past six, the doorbell rings. Mr and Mrs Bell are on the doorstep, anxious to get at the food and drink before anybody else. They know you have to start early if you are going to get five pounds'-worth of wine and gherkins inside you.

'Good evening, vicar,' they say in chorus, and push past him into the kitchen where most of the feast is spread out. 'Are we the first?'

'Come in, come in,' John Elliott says, but his welcome is somewhat redundant because, before he has even closed the door, they have shucked off their coats and helped themselves to a glass of wine and a pickled onion. Christine comes down the stairs and gives a convincing show of delighted surprise to see the Bells. The couple are in their sixties and he is deaf. But Christine is very good on these occasions. Within a minute, she is deep in conversation with Mrs Bell, while the vicar is attempting to engage Mr Bell.

'Is it cold enough for you, Mr Bell?' he asks.

'What's that?'

Before the vicar can repeat the question, Mr Bell's attention has moved on to the tray of pork pies on the kitchen table. He picks one up and sniffs it suspiciously, as if it might have rat poison in it. He bites it.

'Did you get these pork pies at Tesco, vicar?'

'I believe I did, yes.'

'You can get the same thing at Aldi for ten pence a packet less. You might remember I said so, next time.'

Before the vicar can think of how to answer this remark, with its insinuation that he has been extravagant with church funds, the doorbell rings again and he excuses himself. Two more couples wait outside. By a quarter past six, the little house is filling up. There are, of course, the sixteen regular members of his congregation, but also quite a few hangers-on who turn up for these occasions even if they never make it to church. The more the merrier, the vicar thinks; they might be on course to make a couple of hundred pounds for the evening. The bottles of wine are being consumed with alarming rapidity and the vicar is worried that the food and drink might run out before he has sold all the raffle tickets.

He does his best to keep the conversation going, but it is difficult to talk to people, keep their glasses filled and hand food around all at the same time. He's never at ease on these occasions. His wife is the one with the social skills. Christine is selling raffle tickets now, so in a quarter of an hour or so they will be able to have the draw. After that, it is just a question of how long it will take to get their guests out of the door again.

Martha Taylor, who sometimes helps with the flower arrangements in the church, corners the vicar in the living room.

'A lovely party, vicar,' she says.

John Elliott can't think of anything to say. He doesn't think there is anything lovely about this particular party, but he daren't speak his mind. Perhaps this is another reason why he is unsuited to his present job. Martha Taylor already looks as if she's worried she might have said something to upset him.

'Thank you,' he replies. 'By the way, Martha, do you remember our previous vicar here, the Reverend Alfred Stone?'

'Oh, Alfred. Yes, of course I remember him. What made you ask?'

'I went to see him in hospital the other day.'

'Really?' Martha Taylor's face shows genuine curiosity. 'How was he?'

'Not very well.'

'Oh dear me. I'm sorry to hear it. He was a very nice man. Older than you, of course, but for a long time he was just like any vicar. Just like you, in many ways. No surprises. We don't like surprises in this parish. We're rather set in our ways here.'

'So what happened?' asks John Elliott.

'He went all holy. Forgive me, John, I know vicars are meant to be religious people. But Alfred started to get very worked up about things. He started to preach at us. Well, we all like a sermon, but we like a short sermon better. We like your sermons, John. We don't always understand what you're on about, but at least they're short.'

'And his weren't?'

'No they were not. He started to preach about hellfire and damnation. Well, who wants to hear about that sort of thing in this day and age? When he invited us to take Communion, to eat the flesh and to drink the blood, it was the way he said it. As if he really believed it was the actual flesh and the actual blood. It quite put me off.'

On the small table next to where they are standing, there is a phone. Now it starts ringing. John Elliott excuses himself and picks up. He asks who is calling, but the background noise in the room is terrific, so it is hard to hear.

'I'm sorry, am I calling at a bad time?' asks the woman.

'No, not at all. A few friends have dropped in for a drink. Who is calling?'

'I thought I ought to let you know that Alfred Stone died this morning. Heart failure.'

He recognises her voice now. It is Dr Mindrum from St Mark's.

The vicar finds a chair and sits down.

'I'm terribly sorry to hear that,' he says. Laughter and loud conversation render his remark inaudible to Dr Mindrum, so he has to repeat it.

'It was probably a relief,' she tells him. 'The poor man was in a very distressed state last night, as you saw. It only got worse after you left. The sedation didn't help for very long.'

'Oh dear. I don't seem to have done him any good.'

'Thank you for coming. It was kind of you. It was worth a try and it obviously meant something to him. He kept talking about you after you'd left. He seemed to think there was someone who was in danger, and only you could help.'

'Well, yes. I don't know what all that was about.'

As he says this, John Elliott is conscious that it is very close to an untruth. He suspects he knows exactly who the mad priest was asking him to protect.

'I thought you'd want to know,' says Dr Mindrum.

'Thank you for ringing.'

'I'd better let you get back to your party.'

They hang up. John Elliott remains seated in his chair for a moment. He hadn't done any good. Yet again, he's tried and failed. Christine is beside him opening another bottle of red wine. She says fiercely, 'Come on, I can't do it all on my own.'

189

'Sorry,' says her husband, rising to his feet.

'You'd better make your speech, and then we can draw the raffle tickets. We're running low on wine.'

The vicar goes into the living room where most of the guests are crammed together. He finds an empty wine glass and tings it with a fork until he has something like silence.

'Friends, thank you,' he says. Old Mr Bell can be heard complaining about the shortage of pickled onions. 'Thank you,' says the vicar in a louder voice.

He makes his customary speech. They've all heard it many times. He thanks them for their diligence in attending church. 'Without you, the bishop would have to close us down.' The laugh he always follows this remark with sounds a little forced, even to his ears. He enjoins those in the room who have just come along for the party to attend next Sunday's service. 'Give us a try.' He makes some announcements: there is to be a young people's dance the night before Christmas Eve. There will be a coffee morning at the vicarage next Wednesday for the Friends of St Joseph's, and everyone is invited to bring along someone who hasn't been to the church before. He says it is not too soon to begin rehearsals for the carol service on Christmas Eve.

He knows all of these events will be sparsely attended. If they don't start selling tickets for the dance soon, it will have to be cancelled. Even as he speaks, he wonders why he bothers. Then he stands to one side to allow Christine to draw the winning raffle tickets from a hat.

Once the raffle has been drawn, and the prizes distributed, it is understood that everyone can go. All the drink has gone, and so has most of the food. But life is never that straightforward. A few guests feel that the evening

190

will not be complete until they have stayed on for a cup of coffee and perhaps some biscuits, if the vicar can be prevailed on to hand around the tin of shortbread.

It is nearly eleven o'clock by the time the last visitors have left, and John and Christine Elliott are exhausted. By common consent, they decide to leave the mess downstairs until the next morning. They go upstairs and get ready for bed. As Christine is brushing her teeth, her husband says, 'Oh, by the way, I forgot to tell you. I saw George in the supermarket this afternoon.'

He has to remind his wife who George Mitchell is and goes on, 'He had mountains of tinned food in his trolley. He looked as if he was preparing for an expedition to the North Pole. Of course I went towards him to say hello. And do you know what? As soon as he saw me coming, he turned his face away from me. He cut me dead. Just blanked me. I must have offended him somehow.'

His wife rinses out her mouth and as soon as she can speak again replies, 'Oh well, you always said he was an odd man. I shouldn't give it a second thought.'

They climb into bed and switch off their bedside lamps. Christine asks, 'How did you think it went this evening?'

'About par for the course. Thank you for all your help, sweetheart.'

'Quite something, to think we'll probably be giving parties like that for the next thirty years,' remarks his wife. There's a long silence, and John Elliott feels himself beginning to drift away when Christine asks another question.

'Who was that on the phone earlier this evening?'

'Oh, that was someone from St Mark's.'

'Do they want you to visit that poor man again?'

'No. They rang to say he died this morning.'

'Oh,' says Christine sleepily. 'I'm sorry. Tell me about it in the morning.'

A moment later, small snores are coming from her side of the bed. But John Elliott is wide awake. He thinks for a while about Alfred Stone, and wonders what terrible visions brought him to such an untimely death. He was unable to help Alfred Stone and he is beginning to think that he is unable to help anybody. He thinks he's a failure and that he would be better employed doing almost any other job except that of a parish priest. He slides into an uneasy sleep.

He dreams that he's outside the school again. He senses someone's presence nearby. He turns to face him, and Theo's eyes lock on to his.

'Is that you?' asks the vicar.

Theo says, 'Look at me.'

In his dream, John Elliott turns away and hides his face.

Nine

The next morning they come downstairs and clear a space on the kitchen table amongst the used wine glasses and dirty plates so that they can have breakfast. Christine pours them both a cup of tea and says, 'Do you remember what I said last night?'

Her husband's mouth is full of toast, so he just shakes his head.

'I said, I can't imagine giving drinks parties like the one we had last night for the next thirty years.'

'Oh, you won't have to,' says John Elliott cheerfully. 'Most of the people who were here last night will be dead in thirty years' time. It'll be a new lot by then.'

'You know what I mean. Anyway, if the next generation is going to take over, why aren't they coming to church now?'

Her husband looks at her as if she has slapped him. His good humour vanishes. He says, 'You know I'm doing my best to bring new people into the congregation.'

'Yes, and I'm doing my best to help you. It just isn't working.'

John Elliott stands up. 'I must be going – and so must you. It's half past eight.'

'John,' says Christine. 'We really need to talk about this. You're in a dead end here. It will burn you up if you don't do something about it.'

He pulls on his coat and says, 'We'll discuss it some other time.'

John Elliott leaves the house, slamming the door behind him. Then he realises he has nowhere to go. That afternoon he has home visits to make around the parish, but this morning was to be spent in the house, clearing up the mess from the previous night. That's the bargain. Christine will help with social evenings, coffee mornings and all sorts of other events – church fetes, flower displays, quiz nights – but he has to do the tidying up afterwards. She hasn't the time during the school term.

He would look foolish going back into the house now and, in any case, a walk will do him good. He feels tired after the events of the previous two nights, and he's got a headache. The cold air revives him as he enters the lane towards St Joseph's. He turns aside at the wicket gate and walks up the path to the church and around the side to see whether the repairs to the roof have started. They haven't. A ladder is lying on the ground and there are a few other traces suggesting the recent presence of workmen but, as usual, nobody is actually doing anything.

He retraces his steps, unlocks the main door and goes into the church, flicking on the lights as he passes through the porch. He walks to the front of the church and sits in a pew. For over one hundred Sundays he has stood at that lectern, delivering – as he supposed – the word of God to the same sixteen people. Is he any better for all that effort and all those words? Are they? It's as if the church, and its congregation, has been frozen in time, unchanging, no longer really alive.

He stands up and surveys his kingdom: the stained-glass windows in which the colour has been subdued by

194

deposits of soot on the outside; the uncomfortable and narrow pews; the cracked plaster on the walls; the smell of dust with overtones of dry rot.

This place is dead.

Maybe Christine is right, he thinks as he walks back to the door. Maybe I should quit while I can, before I become embedded in this building, an unemployable vicar who couldn't do his job. If I leave now, maybe people will give me the benefit of the doubt: a young man who picked the wrong career, but hasn't left it too late to find a different path.

He goes outside and walks round the side of the church to wander amongst the gravestones. Which was the grave marker that poor Alfred Stone saw in his hallucination? He walks across the patches of frozen snow and finds a gravestone laid flat. It is partly obscured by snow and frost, but the engraved legend, reporting the name of the occupant below and the date of death, is illegible. Time and the weather have blurred the inscription. Isn't this the corner of the churchyard where he saw Mary Constantine standing?

His mind begins to speculate feverishly, against his own will. He struggles to block out these thoughts and returns to the path, and then to the house to clear away the remains of last night's party. Hard work is the best way to shut down the imagination.

In a couple of hours, the house is looking tidier. He puts the bin bags of litter and the empty bottles into the boot of the car and takes them down to the waste-reception centre in Hexham.

On the way back, he checks his watch and sees he has a few minutes to spare before the first of his afternoon appointments. He's just got time. It's ten days to Christmas and both Christine and he have been too busy to do anything about it. He hasn't even thought about a present for her. He drives into a garden centre near the main road, and emerges a quarter of an hour later with a small and scruffy-looking spruce: a Christmas tree. He's also managed to buy some glass globes and a string of fairy lights. It will be a surprise for Christine. She'll love it. And it will make the house a little less bleak.

His home visits are not a success. He doesn't limit these to members of his congregation. He visits the sick and the lonely in his parish. He thinks of himself as an ambassador for St Joseph's, although none of his visits ever increases the attendance at his church. He tells himself this doesn't matter. It is his Christian duty to visit these people, and maybe one day he will penetrate their indifference. Three out of the four people he'd telephoned in advance to say he was coming are out. The fourth, an old lady called Mrs Macdonald, is in, but she has her television turned up to the maximum volume. When the vicar arrives, she makes no effort to switch it off or turn it down. He sits and chats to her for ten minutes, and it is clear she cannot hear a word he says. *He* cannot hear a word he says. The visit is less than satisfactory, and he leaves as soon as he can. Mrs Macdonald's eyes swivel back to the television screen as soon as he stands up to go. She has scarcely taken in the vicar's presence in her sitting room.

As he gets back into his car, his mobile rings, and all hell breaks loose.

It's Christine. She tells him he needs to come to Temple School as soon as possible.

'The police are here. They want to speak to you,' she tells him.

'The police? Why do they want to speak to me?'

In his mind he's trying to think what it could be: has he been speeding? Has someone died? He works it out just as Christine tells him, 'It's Theo again.'

'What's happened?'

'Just get here as soon as you can.'

His drive to the school would certainly capture the attention of any passing police car, but fortunately he doesn't meet one. Christine is waiting anxiously at the entrance to the school, and together they hurry to the gym block.

'Is he all right?' asks John Elliott as they cross the playground.

'No, of course he's not all right. You'll see.'

Once again, but this time with a sense of dread, he enters the gym block and follows Christine to the changing rooms. There is the headmistress and Griffith Jones, and another civilian: a lady in a tweed suit. She is frowning as John Elliott enters the room. She looks as if she frowns a lot. Besides these people, there is a uniformed police officer and Dr Carter. Theo is lying on a bench. As before, his pullover and shirt have been removed. The headmistress starts to speak, to explain to the rest of the room who John Elliott is, but he ignores her and hurries over to Theo.

The overhead lights in the changing room are dull, as if not enough power is getting through to them. But, even so, John Elliott can see that this time the wounds are awful. There is a gash in Theo's left side and blood is trickling from wounds in his palms and feet. Blazing red lacerations appear on his forehead and disappear under his hair. Beneath the lacerations, Theo's eyes are open. He is calm. He shows no pain. His gaze is remote. It has an implacable quality to it.

197

His eyes lock onto John Elliott's and hold his gaze. The vicar is so shocked, he cannot move. Then he finds his voice: 'Who did this to you, Theo?'

John Elliott is oblivious to the other people in the room, but the headmistress interrupts: 'Let's leave the questions to the police, shall we, Mr Elliott?'

John Elliott turns from Theo with reluctance and endures introductions to Sergeant Bellingham and Mrs Allen, the lady in the tweed suit, who is introduced as a social worker. Mrs Allen looks at him with old-fashioned disdain as they are introduced. The formalities over, the vicar turns to the doctor and asks: 'Is he in pain?'

'Amazingly enough, he doesn't appear to be,' says the doctor. 'His pulse and temperature are normal. I wanted to give him morphine, but he refused it.'

Nobody remarks on how odd it is that a child of nine can tell a doctor what he can or can't do.

At this point, the headmistress breaks in. It's her meeting; her agenda; her school.

'Now, I hope you all understand that I and my staff are quite clear these injuries weren't inflicted by anybody at this school. Christine?'

Christine agrees.

'We noticed the injuries about two hours ago, when Theo was changing for football.'

'I called in Dr Carter, and notified the police the instant I heard,' says the headmistress.

'So who is responsible for these marks on the boy?' asks Sergeant Bellingham.

Dr Carter starts to reply, but the headmistress interrupts and speaks for him instead.

'Dr Carter says these marks were made by one or more sharp instruments, like a knife, or a nail. Isn't that so, Dr Carter?'

'Yes, although I don't know what made the scratches on his forehead.'

'Could one of the children have attacked the boy with a knife?' suggests Sergeant Bellingham.

'Of course not! How absurd! Children of nine years of age?' The headmistress directs her most intimidating look towards the policeman, but he continues his line of enquiry: 'Or one of the older boys or girls?'

Christine says, 'Theo's in my class. I've been with him most of the day. We've been doing rehearsals for the Christmas play. None of the children played outside at lunchtime. It was too cold. I can't imagine how anyone could have found an opportunity to hurt Theo without being seen.'

John Elliott looks at the others in the room. He can't believe that they are sitting here in the children's changing rooms discussing where to fix the blame, while a boy lies bleeding on one of the benches.

'Has anyone called an ambulance?' he asks.

'He's in no immediate danger, and he doesn't appear to be in pain,' replies Dr Carter.

'We need to get the parents here to see Theo and explain to us how he came by these injuries,' explains Mrs Allen.

Griffith Jones interrupts, 'We need to interview the parents as soon as possible,' he says. 'This is a classic case of domestic violence.'

'I'm afraid this is my case,' says Mrs Allen. 'We will let you know if your services are required when we know a little bit more about the circumstances in which this child met with these injuries.'

'Is there any possible doubt? It must have been the parents who did this,' replies Griffith Jones. A row seems to be about to break out between these two, but Sergeant Bellingham interrupts them to say that a car has been sent to pick up the parents. He stands up and walks across to Theo. The boy is sitting up on the bench now. To John Elliott's eyes, the wounds on his hands and feet and face and side now appear to be a little less angry. He looks up as the policeman approaches.

'Who did this to you, Theo? We need to find out so we can stop it happening again.'

No answer. Theo looks at the policemen and then smiles for a moment.

'Was it your mother? Or your father?'

No answer.

'Does your father get angry sometimes? Does he hit you?'

At last Theo replies. 'My father's anger can be terrible.'

Sergeant Bellingham turns to the headmistress. 'Is he saying his father did this?'

'I've no idea,' replies the headmistress. 'But George Nixon is his stepfather, not his father. Mary Constantine is his mother and Mr Nixon lives with her and Theo.'

Dr Carter says, 'Look! The marks on his body are fading. Just like last time.'

Everybody looks at Theo. The strip lighting in the changing rooms makes a buzzing sound, flickers and goes off for a moment. Then it comes back on. It is dark and then it is light again, and in the light that now blazes from the neon tubes, everybody can see that the marks on Theo's body have gone.

'Is this some kind of joke?' asks Sergeant Bellingham,

addressing the room in general. Theo nonchalantly puts on his grey shirt and pullover. The vicar notices blood-stains on the shirt.

'It's no joke,' says the headmistress. 'Nothing could be less funny. We all saw the wounds.'

'I would swear to them in court,' adds Griffith Jones. The sergeant asks Dr Carter, 'Can you explain any of this?'

'I know what I'd say if I were a priest, and living in the sixteenth century,' says Dr Carter.

'How is that relevant?' asks the headmistress.

'What would you say in that case?' asks John Elliott.

'I'd say the wounds were stigmata.'

John Elliott hears the very word he had used to describe what had happened to Theo when he went to meet Dr Blair. The word he has wondered about ever since; the idea he has tried to dismiss as fantasy. Stigmata. *I bear on my body the marks of Jesus* says St Paul. John Elliott knows that the doctor must be right. But in his training at theological college, he can only recall reading about the stigmata of saints and martyrs. He has never heard about it happening to a nine-year-old child. In which case, who is this child? *What* is this child?

It isn't clear if anybody else in the room understands the word. If they do understand it, nobody is taking any notice. Sergeant Bellingham asks, without a trace of irony, 'And what would you say if you *weren't* a sixteenth-century priest?'

Dr Carter replies, 'These injuries must have been inflicted at some time by a person, or persons. I can't account for their disappearance. Maybe what we have been seeing is an extreme psychosomatic event: the body somehow recapitulating the events of a previous trauma.'

201

Sergeant Bellingham looks dissatisfied. 'I don't know what more the police can do,' he says. 'We'll interview the parents when they arrive. But without physical evidence, we're a bit stuck when it comes to establishing that an assault has taken place.'

At that moment, the door of the changing room opens. In comes a police constable, followed by Mary Constantine.

Ten

Mary Constantine at once rushes to Theo and puts her arms around him. 'Theo,' she says. 'Have you been hurt? Are you all right?'

Theo looks up at his mother and smiles. The look tells her everything is fine, she's not to worry. His expression is so peaceful it calms her down.

'I was so worried about you when the police came to collect me.'

'I feel fine,' Theo tells her. 'Can we go home now? I'm hungry.'

Mary lets go of Theo and addresses Sergeant Bellingham.

'Why was I brought here? I was just about to walk up to the school to collect Theo anyway. What was all the panic about?'

'If I can explain . . .' the headmistress begins, but Mary talks over her.

'And who are all these other people? Why are the police here? Why is the vicar here?'

The headmistress tries again. 'When Theo came into the changing room, we noticed he had injuries to his hands and feet, and on his tummy.'

'What injuries? Where?'

Mary picks up each of Theo's hands and looks at them

in turn. Both hands are unmarked. He has been putting his socks and shoes back on, but she takes them off again. She sees no marks on his feet, not even a bruise. She says to the headmistress, 'I can't see any sign of injuries. When did this happen?'

Dr Carter says, 'Nevertheless, there were injuries. I took photographs of them the last time it happened . . .'

'You mean this has happened before? Why wasn't I told?'

Everybody begins to talk at once, except for John Elliott who is still watching Theo. The headmistress, Christine, Mrs Allen and Griffith Jones all talk over each other. Theo smiles at John Elliott when he sees his stare. Then Sergeant Bellingham holds up a hand and says in a loud and commanding voice, 'Could we have a bit of hush here? This is getting us nowhere.'

There is a moment's silence as Sergeant Bellingham asks Mary, 'Have you seen any marks on the boy before? At home?'

With reluctance, Mary replies. 'We've seen odd marks on him that we couldn't explain. Twice, at bathtime.'

'Where on his body were these marks?' asks the policeman.

'On his hands and feet both times. Once on his back and side too.'

'Did you see scratches on his face?' asks Dr Carter.

'I'll ask the questions here, if you don't mind,' says Sergeant Bellingham, but Mary answers anyway. 'Never on his face. And all the marks disappeared quite quickly. We thought he might be being bullied at school, but he said not. Didn't you, darling?'

'There's no bullying at Temple School,' says the head-mistress angrily.

204

'Nobody would bully Theo,' adds Christine. 'He's everybody's pet.'

'How do you think he got those marks, Mrs Constantine?' asks Sergeant Bellingham.

'Was it the father?' interrupts Griffith Jones. 'Does he have an anger problem? Does he drink? Does he use drugs? Have there been any other forms of abuse?'

Mary ignores this.

'We don't know what caused the marks. They never seemed to last long enough for us to need to take Theo to the doctor. He wasn't in pain.'

Sergeant Bellingham scratches his head. He doesn't know what to do. He is used to dealing with cases of assault and domestic violence. He isn't quite sure what he's meant to do when the evidence disappears like smoke, right in front of him. At last he says, 'I need to talk to you and your partner about this, Mrs Constantine, but not here. Take the boy home now. What time is Mr Nixon usually home from work?'

'He should be home by seven.'

'I'd like to come and have a quiet talk with both of you later on. I'm not interviewing you under caution. Not just yet. I need to get a better understanding of what's been going on.'

Mary nods her head unwillingly.

'I want someone from the school to be present at any interview,' says the headmistress. 'Theo is our pupil and we have some responsibility here.' Everyone knows that she means she doesn't want the interview to reflect badly on her school.

'You've made an allegation of assault,' Sergeant Bellingham tells her. 'It's my job to investigate it. Not yours, nor anybody else's. If we decide there is a case to answer, we will notify the school, and social services.'

'Can we go now?' asks Mary Constantine. The policeman nods. Theo takes his mother's hand and says, 'Goodbye, Mrs Elliott. Goodbye, Mr Elliott.'

When they are gone, Sergeant Bellingham asks John Elliott, 'I'm told you've seen this sort of thing once before. Would you tell me about it?'

The vicar describes the first time he saw marks on Theo's hands, the bloodstains where Theo had fallen against a bank of snow.

'Why didn't you inform the school? Or the police?'

'Because the marks faded almost as soon as I noticed them. Much faster than this time. Nobody else saw them. I couldn't prove even to myself that I hadn't imagined the whole thing.'

Sergeant Bellingham looks unhappy. Without saying anything further, he leaves the room.

'There's no smoke without fire,' Griffith Jones tells everyone who is left. 'We all saw what we saw. The parents did it. Or one of them did it. It's usually the father, isn't it, Mrs Allen?'

Mrs Allen looks at him without affection.

'Statistically, that is right. We must presume domestic violence has occurred, but I am a long way from understanding how these injuries can present themselves so vividly, and then disappear.'

Dr Carter shakes his head with the air of a man who has decided this is one problem he is going to stay well away from.

'I haven't a clue how that could happen,' he says. 'I'm a GP, not a neuroscientist.'

The meeting breaks up in some disarray. The two social workers leave and the headmistress stands up and says to Christine, 'I want to talk to you about the Christmas play. Come to my office with me for a moment.'

John Elliott is left on his own. The changing rooms have ceased to be a stage on which, in his opinion, a miracle has just occurred. Now they are just changing rooms again: white walls, wooden benches, football strips hanging on one or two hooks where they have been forgotten, a faint smell of children; milk and ammonia.

He decides he needs fresh air. He knows he has to make up his mind about Theo, or he will never have another day's peace. Has Theo been afflicted by some unknown psychiatric illness, which produces symptoms indistinguishable from raw injuries to his body? That is unlikely enough. But what possible alternative explanation is there?

The alternative offered by Dr Carter, the explanation he thinks might have been offered by a superstitious sixteenth-century mind, is that Theo is exhibiting stigmata: the replication of the five wounds of Christ. It is an idea embraced by the Catholic Church, but not by the Church of Scotland or England. It has been bundled together with other supposed 'miracles': weeping statues of the Virgin Mary, visions and other mystical phenomena. A priest who claimed that one of his parishioners was exhibiting these marks and that the marks came and went, leaving no medical evidence that they had ever existed – what sort of reaction could he expect?

John Elliott already has an idea of how his former tutor, Dr Blair, would treat the suggestion. His bishop, a kind and gracious man, might not permit himself the mixture of incredulity and contempt that Dr Blair showed when John Elliott tried to talk to him about the marks he had seen on Theo. But would he be prepared to go out on a limb and support the vicar, should he ever find the courage to make such an extravagant claim as this? It doesn't seem likely. It doesn't seem likely at all.

And what about the press? They would be all over this. They would besiege Theo at his school and Mary Constantine in her flat. They would doorstep John and Christine Elliott at their vicarage. He could imagine the headlines: 'Tyne Vic Sees Marks of Crucifixion on School Pupil'. Underneath, the killer subheading: 'Expert says photographs are faked; school denies any knowledge.'

It would kill him. It would kill Christine. She'd probably lose her job. The headmistress was bad enough on a good day. If she saw her school linked in the tabloids to a story like this, she'd go ballistic. There'd be blood on the walls, and it wouldn't be Theo's.

His wife would suffer. *He* would suffer. His congregation would decide he'd become too 'holy', as Martha Taylor had put it. He'd end up with a congregation of zero, and the diocesan administrators and accountants would decide that St Joseph's had become 'unviable'. He's already sensed that word is in their thoughts, if not yet on their lips.

And what about Theo? Could he really expose an innocent nine-year-old boy to the consequences of such a suggestion? That a nine-year-old boy from nowhere was displaying signs of crucifixion? He would be branded as a freak. He would have to leave the school – and where could he go where he was not marked down for derision, and for bullying?

For John Elliott to reveal what he knew – what he thought he knew – about Theo would be the worst possible decision he could take. If his bishop were in front of him now, he would have to deny any such interpretation as stigmata for the wounds that had been seen on Theo's body. He would have to go along with the dreadful Griffith Jones and his colleague Mrs Allen. He would have to say that, however unlikely it might seem, the injuries to Theo were the result of some form of child abuse. It wasn't his job to speculate on why the marks didn't persist longer than they did. He was a vicar, not a doctor and certainly not a neuroscientist, as Dr Carter had put it.

I must be mad to consider the possibility of stigmata for even a moment, thinks John Elliott, shaking his head vigorously, like a dog trying to shed water from its coat. What would that make Theo? A saint? Or something more?

He has continued walking as he conducts this interior debate. Now he is standing halfway up the lane, at the entrance to the church of St Joseph's. Beside the gate is a plaster image of Christ nailed to the cross, affixed to a backboard and under a small steepled roof. Above the plaster figure are the words: 'Iesus Nazarenus Rex Iudaeorum'.

Someone has knocked the figure's head off and scrawled a four-letter word in red ink at its base.

'Bastards,' mutters the vicar to himself, as he hurries along the lane to his home.

Eleven

The weather warms up. Cars slither, and their tyres crackle on the last of the brown slush. As the frost retreats, interesting leaks appear in the Elliotts' bathroom plumbing, which have to be dealt with. John Elliott throws himself with renewed energy into the St Joseph's Church Christmas Dance. This is to be held the night before Christmas Eve. The town hall is hired, as are chairs and glasses. A DJ is on standby – a band is beyond the reach of the vicar's budget. So far, eleven tickets have been sold.

Christine and John Elliott spend an evening in the church, aided by Martha Taylor. Sprigs of holly are tied around the stone pillars. A spray of winter-flowering viburnum is stuck in a vase. A nativity crib is taken out of storage and dusted down and placed at the steps of the altar. When the vicar stands back and surveys the decorations, he cannot derive much satisfaction from their efforts. Somehow the church seems even gloomier than before. But they can't afford proper Christmas decorations.

In between these tasks, the vicar is preparing the hymns and carols for the Christmas services, and discussing them with the organist, an elderly lady with severe arthritis in her hands. All this activity keeps him busy. He blocks out thoughts of Theo as best he can. Thank God there have been no further 'miracles' of the kind he has now witnessed three times at the school. It is all some sort of bizarre trauma the poor child is experiencing, and therefore nothing to do with the vicar or his church.

It is nearly the end of term, and the school Christmas play is due to take place that evening. John Elliott has promised Christine he will come and support her. The subject matter of the play, in conformance with the headmistress's desire not to offend religious or ethnic minorities, is secular and not Christian. There is no question of children dressing up as the Three Kings, with cotton wool beards and spangled robes. There is no room for a crib, no room at the inn and certainly no room at the school for anything in any way reminiscent of the Christmas festival.

The play is put on in the school assembly hall, which has a raised stage with steps leading down to the floor on either side. A makeshift pair of curtains has been rigged up. The theme of the play is in some way related to a giant toyshop. The children have to choose presents that they know will please their friends. Christine is the play's director. The headmistress has written the script, which the vicar has read. He thinks it is clunky beyond measure, but perhaps it will be all right on the night. Aisha, an enchanting eleven-year-old girl of Pakistani descent, is playing the lead role. She will act the part of the girl who finds the key to the shop and lets the other children in. Theo is one of many children who will invade the shop, while an older boy plays the part of a policeman who warns the children that they must pay for everything they take.

There are a number of important messages about civic duty that the headmistress is attempting to get across in the script, but the play seems to be more about retail

211

therapy than anything else. John Elliott arrives in good time, and has the pleasure of watching various children hiding in the wings and taking the occasional peek around the edge of the curtain to see where their parents are sitting. John Elliott sees Theo peer out, and following the direction of his gaze, he sees Mary Constantine sitting a few seats away and in the row behind him. Next to her is a tall, dark-haired man with a pale face shadowed by stubble. This must be Geordie Nixon, the forester who is Mary's partner. He beams with pride as soon as he spots Theo. When Theo's head disappears again, the forester's face resumes the dour expression of a moment before. The vicar suspects this is the normal mask with which Geordie Nixon confronts the world.

Christine is backstage, attending to costumes that have come unpinned, reminding the children of their lines and dealing with the occasional panic attack amongst the smaller members of the cast.

The curtains open, and Aisha Khan comes on and pantomimes opening a door (it is only a doorframe) with a gilded key. The set is minimal, but there has been an effort to convey the impression of the interior of a large shop. The play swings into action and the enthusiasm of the children makes it all work. Theo's part is a minor one. When he appears on stage, the vicar experiences a momentary spasm of alarm, like a cold hand laid on his neck. Will Theo upstage them all, and start bleeding right there, in front of his parents and the whole school? But Theo doesn't. He trots onto the stage and performs his part no worse than any other child in the cast.

At the end of the play, all the children line up at the front of the stage, holding hands and chanting a song about giving presents to the poor. As they leave, each of them is given a present of their own. Then they clatter down the stairs that lead from the stage and join their parents, while Christine and the headmistress and other members of staff accept more applause from the audience. As Theo brushes past John Elliott, he sees that the boy is clutching a Kinder egg. In accordance with the headmistress's desire to reward everyone equally, there are prizes for all.

John Elliott goes to the stage and looks up at Christine and her colleagues and says, 'Well done!'

'You liked it?'

'Brilliantly directed and well acted.'

'It'll be an hour or two yet before I can come home,' says Christine. 'I have to help clear up.'

'I could lend a hand,' offers the vicar.

'Better not,' says Christine, rolling her eyes in the direction of the headmistress. 'She's not a member of your fan club.'

John Elliott shrugs and smiles and starts to make his way to the back of the assembly hall. As he approaches the entrance, he finds himself next to Theo and Geordie Nixon in the queue of parents and children trying to leave. Theo is holding Geordie Nixon's right hand in his left. With his right he takes the vicar's hand, and smiles up at him.

'Did you like it, Mr Elliott?'

'Very much.'

'It was fun.'

Geordie Nixon becomes aware that Theo has joined him to a stranger. He glances at the vicar, who introduces himself.

'Aye, the vicar. Our Theo's told us about you.'

Then Geordie, rather unexpectedly, gives a warm smile, removes his hand from Theo's grasp and offers it to John Elliott. They shake. Geordie's hand is hard and rough. John Elliott thinks to himself: this man could never, ever harm a hair on Theo's head. It just isn't possible. Then Mary Constantine appears beside him and greets the vicar too. For a moment the three grown-ups stand and talk about the play, Theo still clutching the vicar's hand.

'Can Mr Elliott walk home with us a little way?' he asks Geordie and Mary.

'Only if he wants to,' replies Mary. She smiles at the vicar, who assents. They set off through the school gate and down the hill. Geordie and Mary are in front, Theo and the vicar behind. Out of the corner of his eye, John Elliott glimpses someone on the opposite side of the road: a man, clad in what looks like a long raincoat. There's something familiar about him, but then the figure disappears behind a parked van and the vicar forgets about him. They walk for a while down the long, dark street. The street lamps in this part of town are quite often faulty and the orange pools of light occur only at random intervals. As they walk, they chat about this and that.

'I'm glad you liked the play,' says Theo.

'Well, even if it wasn't about Christmas, it was still great fun.'

'I was born on Christmas Eve,' says Theo. 'It's not really fair. I only get one present for Christmas and my birthday together.'

'That's bad luck,' agrees John Elliott.

'You'll protect me, won't you, Mr Elliott?' the boy asks. The question takes the vicar by surprise. He is reminded with a start of the words poor Alfred Stone spoke, the

214

last time he saw him before he died: '*You must save him. That's why you have been chosen.*'

With an effort he smiles at Theo. 'Geordie and your mum will look after you best, Theo. Not me.'

The boy lets go of the vicar's hand. He gazes at the vicar who sees in his stare not reproach, but something remote and implacable. The child's gaze has the force of a blow.

The vicar takes a step backwards and raises his arm, as if to ward off something. Theo turns and runs after his parents.

'Come back!' shouts the vicar. But Theo is out of earshot: a small boy running down a dark street, trying to catch up with the rest of his family.

Twelve

John Elliott dreams, and in his dreams he hears somebody speak the words: 'Mene, tekel, upharsin.'

Even in his sleep, he knows where this comes from. He remembers the quotation from the Book of Daniel: the mysterious moving finger that wrote those words on the wall of the chamber of Belshazzar. He remembers too how the enigmatic phrase is rendered in the King James Bible: 'Thou has been weighted in the balances and found wanting.'

The dream shifts. Someone close to him is about to die, and the manner of their death will be very terrible. In the middle of the night, John Elliott wakes himself up screaming.

Christine turns over restlessly in her sleep but, for some reason, she has not awoken. Perhaps he only dreamed that he cried out. The pulse in his temples is thudding and he feels cold sweat on his face and back.

John Elliott feels as if he is on the very edge of losing his mind. He is following the same path as Alfred Stone, who by thinking too much about what he saw and heard – what he *thought* he saw and heard – ended up in a medium-secure hospital for the mentally ill. He sits up in bed, the cobwebs of his dreams trailing all about him with their invisible silken strands.

He has to quit this job. He can't cope with it any longer. If he doesn't leave now, he will risk losing his health and his marriage. He is quite clear about that. He has been offered a choice that he didn't ask for, between belief and reason. He wants to accept both, and the struggle will tear him in half. He has to get away from St Joseph's, get away from Theo, go and live a different life in a different place.

Everything is clear in his mind. He became a priest out of respect for the memory of his father and to comfort his widowed mother. He gave it no more thought than if he had become articled to a firm of solicitors. He thought he probably believed in God, without enquiring too deeply into the nature of belief. He hadn't understood that belief is not a menu. It is absolute, not discretionary. He hadn't understood where that choice might take him. It wasn't what he was meant to do. He chose this path to please other people, not out of any deep sense of vocation.

The sense of horror that awoke him is fading now. After all, it was only a dream. Christine didn't get home until nine and they didn't eat until ten, so he's gone to sleep on a full stomach. It's not the first time he's had bad dreams for that reason. He slowly slides back down into the bed, his head on the pillow once more. Without being aware of the transition, he dozes and then sleeps, then dreams again.

He is back in the dark street where Theo left him. Theo has gone, but there is movement behind the rows of parked cars. It reminds John Elliott of a dog or a wolf. He feels a terrible sense of unease. Then his dreams cease, or else continue unremembered, and for the remainder of the night he sleeps deeply.

In the morning he can't wake up. Christine shakes him awake twice and each time he falls asleep again. He is drugged with sleep. Then she brings him a cup of tea in bed. He can't remember the last time she did that for him, or he for her. The aroma of the tea wakes him at last and he sits up and sips the hot liquid.

'Sorry,' he says. 'I don't know what's wrong with me this morning. I just couldn't wake up.'

'You tossed and turned a lot in your sleep.'

'Did I?'

'Were you having bad dreams?'

'I can't remember,' lies the vicar. He *can* remember, only too well.

'I must go, I'll be late for school. Don't forget, it's the last day of term. I should be back early. Will you be in?'

Her husband clutches Christine's arm. 'When you come back, we have to talk. You're right about this job. I don't think I can carry on with it much longer.'

'I know I'm right,' says Christine. She kisses him on the cheek. 'I must run.'

When Christine has gone, the vicar gets up, taking his time to shave and dress. There is so much he has to do today, and he doesn't feel like doing any of it. He wants to shrug off the huge weight that has settled on his shoulders, but his sense of responsibility gets the better of him. It would have been nice just to abandon everything: his position as a vicar, his responsibilities to the parish, all the Christmas services and events that are still to be finalised. With considerable reluctance, he gets on with his working day.

He sees Christine only briefly in the afternoon, and then has to go out again to conduct an early carol service. The organist has to play everything in the key of C: her stiff

218

fingers can't cope with anything more complicated. Just after the service has started, the door creaks open and someone comes in and sits at the back of the church, out of the range of the candlelight. They are singing 'Hark! The Herald Angels Sing' and the vicar almost loses his place, he is so surprised. It is George; his face in shadow but, undoubtedly, it is George. The vicar thought he had gone away for good. Well before the service ends, the church door bangs shut, and the vicar realises that George has left before he can have a word with him.

That evening, John Elliott returns home to find his wife has gone to bed early. She's always like that at the end of term: absolutely exhausted, as if all the fatigue she's been refusing to acknowledge for the last few weeks has finally overcome her.

The vicar makes himself a sandwich and sits at the kitchen table, composing a letter of resignation to his bishop. It takes him an hour or two, but in the end he has a draft he decides will have to do. It doesn't matter, after all, how many fine words and well-turned phrases he can think of: he cannot conceal the simple truth. He's letting himself down and he's letting everybody else down. By the time he's finished, it is late, and the kitchen table is covered in screwed-up bits of paper. The letter he will send in the morning reads:

Dear Bishop,

It is with deep regret that I am writing today to inform you of my resignation from the position of vicar of the parish of St Joseph's. I am compelled to do this for personal reasons, which I will not trouble you with by describing in any detail. I feel I have failed in my mission here and I believe I am, after all, unsuited to work in the Church of England. I have thought about this step I am about to take very deeply and my decision is final.

I can only apologise for the trouble and inconvenience my action will give the diocese and, above all, for letting down the people, including you, who believed I could do this job.

I propose to leave the position with immediate effect after Christmas, and to surrender the house within the next four weeks, if that is acceptable to you.

John Elliott has no idea what he will do to earn his living now, or where he and Christine will live. He has no idea whether Christine will be able to give up her position at the school just like that. She has urged him to change his job, but he wonders whether she has thought about the consequences.

At breakfast the next morning, he shows Christine the letter. She reads it without comment and then hands it back to him.

'Well?'

'It's the right thing to do. I have to give a term's notice, but I can take a flat somewhere and come up and see you in Kelso at the weekends.'

'Why Kelso?' asks John Elliott in some surprise.

'Because I've already asked Mum and Dad if we can come and live with them for a month or two while we both look for new jobs and somewhere to live. They've been expecting this.'

The vicar looks at his wife in amazement.

'You never told me!'

He doesn't know whether to be angry or relieved.

'I'm so glad you've finally made up your mind,' says Christine. 'I think your job was beginning to make you ill.' She stands up and comes around the kitchen table and puts her arms around him. 'Don't worry, we'll both find work back home. My parents will be thrilled to have us for a while. They'll look after us.'

Buoyed by this news, the vicar finds the courage to post his letter to the bishop. Now that he knows this will be his last Christmas, he manages to find new energy from somewhere and goes about his tasks with more enthusiasm.

The Young Person's Christmas Dance that evening is not a great success: in the end, about thirty people attend and not all of them are by any means young, as the vicar has had to pad out the numbers with members of his congregation. But the fact that it has occurred at all is a triumph of sorts. The vicar is filled with a tremendous feeling of relief: a sense that he is about to go on holiday. From next week he will no longer have to worry about the size of his congregation, or the fabric of his church, or the losing battle to finance the Parish Share. That part of his life will be history. As for the events of the past few weeks, that business with Theo, it has all been very strange. It has been beyond strange, but this too will fade from his memory once he moves to Kelso. He hopes so.

It is Christmas Eve. The roads are busy with shoppers returning from Hexham or Newcastle with last-minute presents and stocking-fillers. Even the little town itself is busier than usual in the morning. The vicar has a carol service at six that evening. He spends the morning writing what he expects will be his last-ever sermons, for the Christmas Eve and Christmas Day services. Christine is out in the car, doing her own Christmas shopping. The vicar hasn't yet bought her a present. He will have to do it at the very last minute.

When he has finished his preparations, it is already early afternoon but he doesn't feel like lunch. He isn't hungry because a sense of unease has been creeping up on him over the last hour or two without him being conscious of it. From one moment to the next, he is struck by a feeling of nausea so intense that he feels he might be physically sick on the spot. He staggers to his feet, feeling ill and unsteady. What is wrong with him? He felt perfectly fine a few minutes ago.

He knows what is wrong in the same instant that he asks himself the question. Theo is in danger. He knows it now. He's known it ever since Alfred Stone warned him. He feels he's always known it. Whatever, *whoever* Theo is, he has to help him.

At that moment he hears a car door slam, and realises Christine has come back. He goes outside and helps her bring in the Christmas shopping, which includes a small turkey. The thought of eating food ever again is hard to contemplate.

'What's the matter, darling?' asks Christine. 'You're as white as a sheet.'

'Never mind,' says the vicar. 'I need the car.'

'Where are you going?'

'It's about Theo. He's in danger.'

'What danger? How could you possibly know that?'

The vicar scoops up the car keys from the kitchen table, where Christine has left them. She has her hand to her mouth. It's obvious she thinks her husband has gone mad. Maybe I have, thinks the vicar, but I've got to go. Without another word to his wife, he leaves the house and gets into the car. He reverses sharply onto the road with a skid and a bump, then sets off down the street.

Halfway down the road, the steering wheel starts to judder in his hands and pull sharply to the left. The vicar realises he must have a flat tyre. It's only the second time since they've owned this car that he has had a puncture, and it has to happen now. He pulls the car into the side of the road and gets out. It is already close to four o'clock and sunset. The sky is a drab grey and a light drizzle is falling.

He finds the spare and the jack and starts the laborious business of changing the wheel. It is not an easy job in the fading light, and his sense of urgency is growing by the minute, making him fumble. At last he gets the job done. His hands are black with grease, but he doesn't take the time to clean them. He sets out on the circuitous route that will take him around the town, past the school and down to the road near to where he thinks Mary, Geordie and Theo live.

He turns into that road, and drives past a row of parked cars and vans. Once again he has the feeling he has glimpsed movement behind one of the vehicles, but the glimpse is so momentary he cannot be sure. Then he is distracted by the glare of headlights in his rear-view mirror as a huge wagon comes into view behind him. What on earth is a big, articulated truck like that doing in a residential street? The truck is far too close, as if the driver wants to force the vicar to pull over or speed up. But there is nowhere to pull over because the roadside is taken up by parked vehicles.

He hears the hiss and squeal of the giant truck's brakes. It is so close behind him that he can make out the three-pointed Mercedes star on the radiator grill in his rear-view mirror. At that moment he sees Theo.

Theo is walking up the street towards him. He is on his own. How could Mary or Geordie let a nine-year-old child out on his own after dark? Theo is carrying something in one hand. It looks like a book. The vicar wants to stop and jump out and talk to Theo. He wants to explain that he will do everything in his power to help and protect him. He wants to warn him never to go out in these streets alone, and in the winter dark. But he can't stop. The truck behind him has come so close to the rear of the little Nissan Note it is almost touching the bumper. There is the blare of the horn as the driver urges the vicar to speed up or get out of the way.

A side street comes into view and the vicar turns into it with a squeal of tyres, the Nissan leaning over on its suspension as he takes the corner too fast. The car rights itself and the vicar does a U-turn, then accelerates, turning back onto the main road and up the hill with hardly a pause to check for oncoming traffic.

He drives with his window open so that he can call out to Theo as soon as he catches up with him. But he doesn't catch up with him. The street is empty. It is a very long street and there is nobody on either side of the road as far as the vicar can see.

His first thought is to go and find Theo's parents, but he's not sure of their address. It is off this street some-where, but he could spend all evening knocking on doors and still not find them. So he'll ring Christine and ask her to give him their address. With a sick feeling he realises that, yet again, he's left his mobile on the kitchen table.

*

He returns home and Christine meets him as soon as he comes through the door. 'Where on earth have you been? What's going on?'

'I need to know Mary Constantine's address.'

'Why? What's happened?'

'There's no time to explain. Just give me their address.'

Christine is now almost as pale as her husband. She goes to the metal filing cabinet in the sitting room where she keeps her school papers, and starts looking. She finds the address at last and writes it down on a piece of paper.

'I must go there at once,' he says. 'I'll explain everything when I return.'

'But you've got a service starting at St Joseph's in twenty minutes.'

The vicar stares at his wife.

'Oh, God. It's Christmas Eve, isn't it?'

He'd forgotten. How on earth could he have forgotten one of the most important nights of the year, the one service he has to give, that he can never, ever miss? He rushes to the bedroom and changes out of his day clothes into his clerical robes, runs downstairs and spends a precious five minutes trying to find his notes for this evening's service. There will be carols and a sermon. Surely Theo must be back home by now? In his haste and in his confused state of mind, the vicar must have missed him. Or perhaps the boy was visiting a friend and went into someone's house for a few minutes. What he'll do, as soon as the service is over, is he'll walk down from the church to the address Christine has given him and check Theo is all right. Just to be sure.

John Elliott rushes out of the house and up the lane, and only just gets to his own church service on time.

He remembers very little about it. He's conscious that this might well be the very last Christmas Eve service he ever gives. He's conscious that George hasn't come, although he was half expecting him. He sees the sixteen pairs of eyes of the congregation watching him without seeing him, hearing him without listening to him. He goes through the motions and joins in the carols and it all seems to take for ever. Even then he can't go. He has to stand at the door of the church and shake people's hands and wish them all a Merry Christmas, and endure being told 'Mind you don't eat too much turkey' almost sixteen times. He'll be seeing most of them tomorrow at Christmas Day Communion. The same jokes will be made all over again.

At last he's free to go.

He reckons it will be quicker to walk than to go back to the house and get the car, so he sets off as fast as he can stride. He wonders if it will be difficult to find the exact address, in a side street just off the main road somewhere. But it isn't difficult. As he approaches the area where Theo lives, he becomes aware of a pulsing flicker of light: a flashing blue light. Then he sees two police cars drawn up across a side street next to a low-rise block of flats. The sight of these almost stops his heart. Something's happened to Theo, something he might have prevented if he had been a more honest and determined man. As he approaches the flats, a police officer climbs out of one of the cars and asks, 'Can I help you, sir?'

'I was on my way to visit Mrs Constantine and her son Theo.'

'Excuse me, vicar, I didn't notice the collar before. You can't go in, I'm afraid. There's been an incident.'

The use of the word 'incident' fills the vicar with horror.

'An incident? What incident?'

'The young lad's gone missing. We have officers conducting a search and we're interviewing the parents. Perhaps you could come back tomorrow, sir?'

'Theo's gone missing? But I saw him, walking up this very street not long ago.'

'How long ago?' asks the police officer. The vicar checks his watch. It's half past seven. 'About two to three hours ago.'

The police officer gives him a look. Two hours is a long time. He makes a show of taking the vicar's name and address in case he needs to take a statement from him, and then turns his back, making it quite clear that the vicar should take himself off.

John Elliott walks slowly home. At last, feeling as if he has been travelling for years on a journey without purpose, he reaches his own front door. Christine is nowhere in view. The kitchen is in darkness. Leaning in the corner he sees the scruffy spruce, still unadorned, that he meant to put up as a Christmas tree. He realises he's forgotten to buy Christine a present.

He sits at the table with his head in his hands, not quite sure that he has the courage to tell her about Theo.

Thirteen

January in the market town of Kelso in the Scottish Borders: showers of sleet falling from grey skies; the River Tweed brown and sullen, close to breaking its banks. When John Elliott is not sitting in his room, he walks about the cobbled streets; he stands amongst the ruins of the abbey; or he walks along the banks of the river. He walks a lot, but never anywhere in particular.

Home is now the spare bedroom in the house of Charlie and Rose, his parents-in-law. They are kind to him and tolerant of his moods. He suspects Christine has briefed them about his state of mind. He has his own door key and Charlie and Rose allow him to come and go as he pleases. He eats with them in the evenings, but keeps himself to himself for the rest of the day. He is supposed to be looking for a job, but what job? Who will employ an unemployed vicar? What other kind of work is he good for? He doesn't even apply for anything. What's the point? He can see Charlie and Rose would like to ask him what his plans are. Of course they don't want to house and feed him permanently. He knows that.

Christine comes north at weekends. He's glad to see her and, at the same time, he resents the fact that she still has a job, still has some meaning in her life. She tries to pretend she doesn't notice it. Things are difficult. They have rows about trivial things.

Christine brings news. The news she brings is that there is no news. The search for Theo has widened across the north of England and into the Borders, but it is as if he never existed. He's vanished. Christine says that the police are beginning to think Theo might have run away. They've fixed on the bleeding, the strange wounds on Theo's body. There's only one explanation as far as they are concerned: child abuse. Christine says she's heard they are looking for Theo in London: checking shop doorways in the West End, looking amongst the homeless and the vagrants sheltering under old railway arches. They don't find Theo.

She tells him that the other schoolchildren in her class are devastated by Theo's disappearance.

'If he was dead, they could go and put flowers on his grave. It's not knowing that they find so hard to take.'

On Sunday nights Christine heads back south to her cheerless little rented flat in order to be in school for eight o'clock the following morning. She's done everything. She's packed up the house and arranged for their furniture and other possessions to go into storage until they find somewhere to live. She's found herself somewhere temporary to live. She's dealt with all the tedious business of moving on her own. She's let her husband have the car so that he can look for work. She's on her own, but she doesn't complain.

Until John Elliott finds a new job, they won't be able to afford anywhere to live much larger than a kennel. In any case, it's not just John Elliott who needs a new job. Christine will have to find work as well. They can only hope that they will find work in the same place.

Towards the end of January, under pressure from Christine, John Elliott goes to see the local GP. The doctor tells him he is suffering from depression. He tells her he is perfectly all right, but this denial is undermined by the fact that he starts to weep as he speaks. Weeping for no reason has become a habit in recent weeks.

'I'm just short of sleep,' he explains. This is true as far as it goes, but he doesn't explain that this is because he doesn't dare fall asleep in case he dreams of Theo. Each night he lies on his bed, staying awake as long as he can, hearing the boy's voice even while he is awake. He hears the boy say things no nine year old should say: 'Thou hast been weighted in the balances and found wanting.'

He sees the child's calm eyes looking into his own.

'I'm going to refer you to a psychiatrist in Edinburgh,' says the GP. 'He's a very good man. He can help you.'

John Elliott has no intention of going to see a psychiatrist. Like many people, he believes mental illness is just another label for his unfitness for work and life in general. If he sees a psychiatrist, he'll be admitting to himself he is useless. But he makes the mistake of telling Christine about the referral the following weekend.

'So what are you doing about it?' she asks him, as they sit in their bedroom, the only place they can talk without being overheard by Charlie and Rose.

'I don't *need* to see a psychiatrist. There's nothing wrong with me.'

'Nothing wrong with you? John, you're not the same man I married. I married someone who was bright and up for it and hard-working. Now all you seem to do is sit around all day and mope. You haven't even tried to look for a job. How can you say there's nothing wrong with you?'

'Have Charlie and Rose been complaining about me?' asks John Elliott, his voice suspicious and sulky at the same time.

'No, but they would have every right to. They can't look after us for ever.'

In the end, he has to give way. He knows Christine is right. Besides, going to Edinburgh will give him something to do. He visits the hospital in Murrayfield and asks for Professor Thornton. He's no idea what to expect: someone with a bow tie and half-moon spectacles, or a middle-aged hippy with a ponytail. What he gets is a sandy-haired man in his early fifties, sitting behind a leather-topped desk. He's wearing a dark suit with a white shirt and a spotted tie. His manner is friendly and relaxed. He looks more like a bank manager, thinks John Elliott.

The consulting room the professor works in is warm and pleasant. There are watercolours hanging on the walls. There is a bookcase stuffed with books, and not just medical texts either. John Elliott can see the titles of what look like novels, and books of poetry. There is a vase of early daffodils on a low glass table, flanked by two armchairs. When John Elliott comes in, the professor stands up and leaves his desk. He motions John Elliott to take a seat in one of the armchairs, and sits down in the other, facing him.

John Elliott doesn't know what to expect from this meeting, but all they do is chat. Of course he doesn't mention Theo. That must remain his secret. He doesn't want this man to think he's completely mental. So they just chat: and John Elliott finds he is talking about the difficulties of his former job and the challenges of his ministry in a town whose population, for the most part, couldn't be bothered with the church. He talks about his wife, and her job at the school, and how she's going to find it hard to give that up. Professor Thornton doesn't ask difficult questions. He doesn't judge. Once he asks whether John Elliott is taking any medication. Then the session is over and, driving back to Kelso, the former vicar feels he has almost enjoyed the meeting. They have agreed to meet again in a week's time.

A week later, and halfway through the session, Professor Thornton says in his mild way: 'You haven't talked to me about Theo Constantine yet.'

'Theo Constantine?'

'It's odd that you haven't mentioned him. The young boy who disappeared around the same time you gave up your position at St Joseph's. He went to a local school – I think you said your wife taught there. Did you ever meet him?'

'How do you know about Theo?'

'Well, when he vanished at the beginning of the month, there was quite a fuss in the papers and on the TV. Then you mentioned your wife taught at the school he'd attended. I'm just curious as to why you haven't mentioned him.'

'Has my wife been talking to you about me?'

'Goodness me, no. You're protected by patient confidentiality, you know. I wouldn't hold conversations about you with anyone, not even your wife, without your knowledge or unless you had given me permission to do so.'

Under gentle probing from the professor, John Elliott finds himself talking about Theo. He doesn't say too much at first, but at the next session a few days later

232

he mentions for the first time the wounds that appeared on Theo. Professor Thornton raises his eyebrows at this. He appears deeply interested and sympathetic and John Elliott ends up by telling him everything, about the wounds that appeared and disappeared, about the dreadful slur of child abuse that has been cast on Theo's family. And, at last, he reaches a point where he can admit his own innermost belief: that Theo was replicating the Wounds of Christ on his body. That Theo was not just a child but something much more.

When the session ends, Professor Thornton says to John Elliott, 'Well, this has been very productive. Thank you for being so frank. It's been extremely helpful.' He consults a desk diary. 'Let's meet again next Friday.'

John Elliott returns to Kelso feeling as if some of the leaden weight has been lifted from his shoulders. That weekend Christine asks him how he's getting on with the professor.

'Quite well, I think.'

'Quite well? Is that all you can say?'

John Elliott shrugs.

'I just feel if I talk about it too much, it might spoil things.'

'So you think he's helping you?'

But he won't answer her.

The following Friday, the session starts in a different way. The professor's secretary serves coffee and biscuits, a first for these meetings. For a minute or two they talk about almost anything but John Elliott. Professor Thornton says, 'Have a biscuit?'

'Thank you.'

'Finest Scottish shortbread,' says the professor with a smile. Then he adds, 'You and your wife don't have any children yet, I think you said?'

'Yes, that's right.'

The professor makes a note. Then he asks a different question.

'These wounds on Theo you say you saw . . .'

'I saw them. Other people saw them. They were real.'

The professor replies, 'And yet they vanished almost as soon as they appeared.'

'Exactly.'

'Doesn't it strike you that either the wounds were an illusion, or the fact that they vanished was an illusion? One or the other must be true, don't you think? Is it possible that they were never there in the first place?'

'Other people saw them too,' repeats John Elliott. 'It wasn't just me.'

The professor looks up at the ceiling. He's silent for a moment. Then he returns his gaze to John Elliott.

'Doesn't it strike you as a strange coincidence that in a town you describe as being quite uninterested in the church – I think you said you had a congregation of sixteen – a miracle should appear in front of your eyes, in the form of Theo?'

The professor expounds his thesis in a calm and courteous voice. John Elliott has merged his worries about his inability to fill his church with worshippers with his worries about his inability to produce a child. Theo, a child who was real enough, had somehow become the locus for these anxieties. The miraculous wounds, the strange ability of Theo to get inside John Elliott's head, were all projections of his desire for evidence that God was real, his need for something to sustain him in his thankless task as a parish priest.

At first, John Elliott resists this explanation. 'Other people saw the wounds,' he repeats. The professor shakes his head.

'That may well be so. Perhaps there were marks on the boy. It's not for me to sit in judgement on a case I know nothing about, but isn't it possible that these marks were the products of a violent assault? That seems to be the line the police are taking, from what I've read in the newspapers. In any case, it is clear that you – and you alone – decided the injuries you were seeing were miraculous. You decided they were stigmata.'

John Elliott shakes his head. He wants to say, that's not how it was. But there is something so seductive about the professor's analysis of the situation. The professor is offering him a way out of his sleepless nights, his terrifying dreams when he does sleep, the fear that he will – like Alfred Stone – end up in a mental hospital. The professor continues: 'And the guilt you so clearly feel for a boy you hardly knew, to whom you had spoken, what, two or three times?' – here the professor glances again at his notes – 'Isn't that transference of the guilt you feel for not having given your wife a child?'

This is not the last session. There are two further meetings with the professor, and John Elliott realises that he is presenting him with a choice. On the one hand he can reject the professor's scenarios and continue down the path he is on towards long-term unemployment; probably divorce; perhaps madness. On the other hand, he can accept what is being offered to him: a way out of his difficulties before they overwhelm him.

To assist his recovery, the professor prescribes Serendipozan. It is a highly effective psychotropic medicine, non-addictive, with few side-effects. It will help you, he tells John Elliott. You will begin to feel less stressed. You will have a much improved chance of a full recovery.

And the Serendipozan does help, to start with. His life begins to assume a veneer of normality once more. His relationship with his wife, which has been sorely tested by his illness, begins to improve.

These changes do not happen all at once. There are more difficult moments with Christine, more restless nights and eerie dreams. But as the weeks pass, John Elliott slowly gets 'better'. He makes an effort to put his life back together again. He starts applying for jobs. He's not fussy about what he takes on. What he needs is hard work, an income, and as soon as possible a place where he and Christine can live and be on their own again. He is offered a job, and accepts it. It's a position as a guide on coach tours of the Borders. It's not a job he would ever have dreamed of doing a few years ago; it's not his next career, but at least it's work. He has to do a bit of reading to prepare himself and he finds there's so much he didn't know about the country he was brought up in.

The great news that spring is that Christine is pregnant. He believes it will be a boy. He knows it will be a boy.

He doesn't think about Theo as much as before. He's no longer part of Theo's story. He doesn't really want to know how that story ends. The Serendipozan does its work, and the demands on his attention courtesy of his new job help as well.

One day he accompanies a party of tourists a few miles south into England, and Kielder, the vast man-made forest that covers so many hundreds of square miles around the English Borders. They park in a clearing by the side of the road, where a nature trail into the forest is signposted. It is a cool, sunny spring morning. Patches of mist hang here and there above the trees. A few of the more energetic members of the coach party are tempted by the sunshine and decide to walk along the first few hundred yards of the trail, into the edges of the forest itself. John Elliott accompanies them, to make sure that nobody gets lost.

And it would be easy to get lost in this forest, thinks John Elliott. The hills in every direction are covered in trees: Sitka spruce, Norway spruce, Lodgepole pine, Scots pine. A dark mass of tangled trees through which paths and roads are cut from time to time, and then disappear again as the trees encroach upon them. The thought ensnares him: in a brief moment he has a vision of himself lost in a dark wood, lost as Theo is lost, strayed from the path, disappeared from the world and unable to find his way back into waking life. He's experienced these moments of disconnection before: maybe it's the Serendizopan. His heart beats too rapidly for a few seconds and then he gets a grip of himself. He's not lost, he's walking along a nature trail with a dozen other people. And if he were lost, he would soon find the way out again.

It doesn't matter. These odd experiences still intrude from time to time, but there's no doubt he's getting better. In the dying months of the year, Christine will give birth to a boy. He'll get a proper job, they will find somewhere to live and life will begin again.

And perhaps, in time, he'll be able to forget about Theo.

TWO
EERIE TALES
OF SUSPENSE

Reading Group Notes

Discussion Points

Breakfast at the Hotel Déjà vu

1 *'You're one of us, now.'*
Those words made Bobby happier than anything else
anyone else had ever said to him.

  Why does Bobby enter politics? Do you think he has a
  vocation and responds to a sense of civic duty? Or does
  he fall in love with the idea of political power?

2 How important is money to Bobby?

3 Do you blame Bobby for fiddling his expenses? How
  much sympathy do you have for Bobby after his public
  humiliation and rejection from the Conservative Party?
  Has reading *Breakfast at the Hotel Déjà vu* changed
  your opinion of the 'expenses scandal'?

4 Bobby cultivates *a persona* of *someone you could trust,*
  someone dependable while still at school. To what
  extend can someone create their own identity? Is this a
  true reflection of self?

5 Bobby claims that he doesn't want to write a *self-*
  congratulatory political biography. Do you believe this?
  Why do you think Bobby is writing his memoir?

6 Bobby and his father are both caught taking money that doesn't belong to them. Do you believe that certain choices and behaviours are predestined by DNA?

7 Bobby views memory as a *wonderful gift* but then writes that it is *treacherous* and decides *we are trapped by our memories*. How can you explain this tension?

8 There are lots of ways to interpret and understand the strange hotel and Bobby's sense of déjà vu. One interpretation could be that Bobby has died and is enduring a kind of purgatory. If this is true, what do you imagine Bobby has to do to escape the hotel? Do you think he reaches any sort of redemption by the end of the story?

Theo

1 *What if it is all true?*

Do you find anything unusual or unsettling about the way in which Paul Torday presents the clergy?

2 John Elliott feels a strong sense of guilt for failing to increase the size of his congregation and for failing to meet financial targets. Where do you think this guilt comes from?

3 Who is George and where do his talents lie?

4 John suffers some vivid and unpleasant dreams throughout *Theo*. To what extent do you see these as a reflection of his troubled conscience? Or do they have another explanation? Do any stand out for you?

5 Christine thinks her husband is a *square peg in a round hole*. Do you agree with her judgement? How suited is John to the priesthood? Does he even believe in God?

6 Do you believe that Theo's wounds are stigmata? Or is there another explanation?

7 Discuss an allegorical reading of the story. Do the names of the main characters suggest roles within the religious tradition?

8 How far do you agree with Professor Thornton's rational explanation for John's experience of Theo? Can psychology provide an answer?

Compare and Contrast

- *Breakfast at the Hotel Déjà vu* opens with a description of a sunny terrace and blue, untroubled skies. By contrast, *Theo* is set in winter and much of the drama happens under black clouds or amidst deep snow. Why do you think Paul Torday has chosen such different settings for his novellas? Can you find any examples of pathetic fallacy? How effective are these?

- Discuss the tension between self-interest and civic duty in *Breakfast at the Hotel Déjà vu* and *Theo*.

- Bobby and John are both public figures but they approach their roles in very different ways. How can you account for this?

- Both Bobby and John have trouble sleeping. Bobby describes the process *not so much sleep as a million memories, fragmented and brilliant*. How does psychology reveal itself through the unconscious? What insights can you gain from interpreting dreams?

- How are letters used in both novellas? Have you ever written something down because it was too difficult to say aloud?

- What impression do you get of Margaret and Christine? Are they in love with their respective husbands? Do they offer unconditional support, or do they expect certain provisions and behaviour in return for their assistance?

- How does Paul Torday create suspense in each novella? Consider his use of flashback scenes, dream sequences and memories.

- Paul Torday uses third person narrators in both stories. To what extent are these narrators objective and impartial witnesses? Do you think you would feel differently about Bobby if *Breakfast at the Hotel Déjà vu* was written in the first person? How would your view of John change if *Theo* was narrated by Christine?

- Both Bobby and John seem to want to escape the past and forget about the choices they've made and the actions they've taken. Do you think they manage to rectify any of their mistakes by the end? Is redemption possible, and if not, what does this suggest about the power of memory and the intrusion of the past into present life?

Suggested Further Reading

Light Shining in the Forest by Paul Torday

The Translation of the Bones by Francesca Kay

The Sense of an Ending by Julian Barnes

The Testament of Mary by Colm Tóibín

The Lighthouse by Alison Moore

Swimming Home by Deborah Levy

Travels With My Aunt by Graham Greene

And for more Paul Torday . . .

Light Shining in the Forest

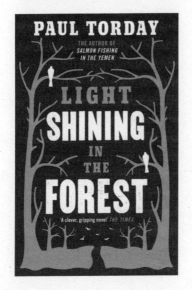

'Excellent . . . well-crafted and constantly gripping'
Daily Mail

'A disquieting and atmospheric psychological novel'
Daily Express

Read on for the first chapter of *Light Shining in the Forest*, a haunting tale about a failing politician and the search for two missing children, featuring one of the most mysterious characters from *Theo*, Georgie Nixon.

One

Kielder Forest lies along the English and Scottish Borders. A few hundred years ago, all this part of the world was a desolation of mires and low, heather-covered hills. Its inhabitants – more then than there are now – were once considered masterless men, who acknowledged no king and lived by violence and cunning. The Border clans were known as 'reivers' and they lived on either side of the Border: in Liddesdale, Teviotdale, Redesdale and Tynedale: clans such as the Armstrongs, Bells, Charltons, Dodds, Elliots, Kers, Nixons and Scotts. They stole from each other and fought with each other. The Border region was difficult for any king to control, whether he was king of Scotland or England. For a while, it was known as the Debatable Land.

It is an empty and silent country. Even today, on this crowded island, there are spaces along the Borders where you can walk for a day without ever seeing another human being.

The country itself has changed. Once there were grey-green hills, covered in rushes and heather. Steep-sided denes scored the hillsides; thick with birch, alder, willow, oak and pine. These ancient woods have now been replaced by a patchwork of huge forests: Wark, Kielder, Redesdale, Harwood, Newcastleton, Craik, Tinnisburn, Spadeadam and Kershope, spread across hundreds of square miles. Tens of millions of trees: Sitka Spruce, Norway Spruce, Lodgepole Pine, Larch, Scots Pine; a dark host only occasionally relieved by avenues of broadleaves. Who lives there now? A few forestry communities, scattered villages and isolated hamlets. Foxes, deer, buzzards, goshawks, jays, magpies, ravens and crows far outnumber the human inhabitants. Once there were red and black grouse living in the heather-clad hills, and grey partridge in the white grassland. But the predators that live among the trees, the hawks and the foxes, have dealt with most of these. Nothing much else lives here; nothing except the trees themselves.

Intersecting the forest is a labyrinth of graded roads. Each year several million trees are planted and as many more are extracted, taken by road down to the chipboard factory in Hexham, or to the Tyne docks, or to the stockyards of timber businesses and fencing contractors. Most of what is logged is softwood, not suited for joinery or cabinet-making, and destined for some industrial purpose. The roads are cut through the forest as they are needed, and then abandoned, chained off to prevent access, quickly overtaken by weeds, and then by regenerating pine and fir. Kielder Forest alone covers two hundred and fifty square miles, and its siblings cover maybe twice that area.

Before the trees came, this was a land of marshes and rolling grass hills. Across the hills ran the old droving roads along which sheep were driven to markets further south, or else to the strongholds of the local clans. The place names recall the former nature of the land and its people: Haggering Holes, Bessie's Bog, Bloody Bush, Foulmire Heights, Gray Mare Moss. The mires and moss were a perfect protection for the reivers who once inhabited this region.

It was a landscape of a thousand soft colours: the subtle shades of heathers, bog myrtle, sphagnum moss, cotton grass,

4

lichens and the whites and browns of the grasslands: an infinitely varied palette, changing with every shift of light from the cloudy, windy skies above. Now only corners of this older world can be glimpsed in places where it has not yet been submerged in the sea of conifers.

Many of the trees were planted in the 1920s as part of a national undertaking to replace timber consumed in the trenches in France during the First World War. Much later, an enormous lake appeared in the forest. It was created by damming the headwaters of the North Tyne – seventeen miles of it between tree-clad banks – to provide water for industry further east. A drowned village lies beneath its waves. As for the trees, it is difficult to know what purpose they now have: they have become an end in themselves, a reason for their own existence. The trees are there because the trees are there.

Geordie Nixon has worked in forestry for most of his life. His father and his grandfather were woodmen. His father tended the private forestry of a local estate. In those days trees were still worth money: ash, beech and oak for furniture; larch was once cropped for ship's masts. Now a tide of cheap timber from Eastern Europe and the former Soviet Union has made home-grown woodlands close to worthless. His father was made redundant and died young, aged sixty. His mother died a few years later, still working as a cleaner.

Geordie began by helping his father during the school holidays. When he was sixteen, he left school and started work as a fencing contractor. He's done fencing, planting, weeding amongst the young trees. Now he's registered as a lone worker and he harvests the trees in Kielder for the Forestry Commission.

He has known nothing else. He visits Hexham, the nearest

town of any size. He's been to Newcastle, the nearest city, twice. He's never been to London, and has no plans to go there. He barely knows where London is. What he does know is the forest, and the birds and the animals that live there. Almost every day he sees the deer lifting their heads to look at him as he drives deep into the forest in his truck. In their season he hears the vixens shouting. He knows where the badger setts are. From time to time, he hears the scream of a rabbit being taken by a hawk. These sounds and shapes and sights are his company when he works in the forest. He works in all weathers: in the faint sunshine that sometimes filters down through the trees; in driving rain; sometimes in the soft and soundless fall of snow, when the forest seems to go to sleep under its white blanket.

You don't find men like Geordie Nixon in towns. You find few men like Geordie anywhere. He's a big man, over six feet tall, and he looks as tough as the trees he cuts down. He has a square, pale face and grey eyes under thick black eyebrows.

His life is work. The money comes in and it goes out even faster. Geordie knows he won't die a rich man. He doesn't think much about the future. He knows he has to meet the lease payments on his vehicles and his HP on the forty-inch HD television in the flat. He has to pay his girlfriend, Mary, his share of the rent on her flat, and his share of the food and heating. He owns nothing except the clothes he stands in, his chainsaw and his mobile phone.

At first light, Geordie Nixon is working with the chainsaw and is already well into the area of forest marked out for clear-felling. He cuts away the small trees and other bits of rubbish to allow the harvester to reach the bigger trees that have to be felled and logged. By eight-thirty, he is cutting down trees in his harvester, a second-hand Valmet 941. It is tracked, to cope with the soft ground. Rubber tyres would just dig in and sink. The whole of this forest grew out of bottomless mires, or else fell land full of sharp rocks.

Geordie is contracted to cut down a block of thirty-year-old Sitka Spruce. The harvester grinds and chugs and whines as its hydraulically powered jaws grab a tree and then bite into its base. In a few seconds the tree has been cut, but it is not allowed to fall: instead the harvester tilts the tree over in its jaws and strips off the branches and most of the bark, then cuts it to length before placing it on top of a growing pile of poles beside the forest track.

Geordie works alone. It's what he prefers. There isn't the money in the job to pay the wages of another man. Once he would have had a lad helping with the stacking of the felled timber, so that he didn't have to load up his truck at the end of the day. Now he has to do it himself. But even Geordie knows about market forces. He's seen the price of timber go down year after year.

Every now and then, he stops to take a nip of lukewarm tea from his Thermos, or else to light a cigarette. When he switches off the engine of the harvester, the silence of the forest is uncomfortable. At midday he stops again and eats the packed lunch – his 'bait', he calls it – that Mary has put up for him the night before: processed cheese slices in a bap, with not enough butter. He eats the dry food mechanically, and swallows the last of his tea. Although it is only early April, there is a hatch of midges. These trouble him whenever he opens the door of the cab. Around him a soft light filters through the forest canopy: a hint of the sun far above the clouds, just enough to gleam on the wet cobwebs on every branch, on the wet bracken by the edge of the wood, on the pools of water lying everywhere. From his cab, Geordie can see down into the

7

shallow valley on whose upper slopes he is working: nothing but spruce and pine, nothing but trees in their endless dark tangles. The light turns greyer in the afternoon as the cloud thickens. Dusk comes early to these places: beneath the shadow of the trees it never really leaves.

At four o'clock he locks up the harvester and walks down to the forest track where he's parked his truck. This is a big Scania tractor-trailer, with a jib-crane at the back for loading up the timber. That and the harvester are leased to him by a finance company.

He has a girlfriend, Mary, whom he thinks of as his 'lass'. Once they had a child as well.

He begins loading the stacked timber from the roadside onto his truck. This is a hard task that requires patience: stack it badly, and it might start rolling and then the whole trailer could tip over. After an hour or more, he's finished the job and he's finished too. He's absolutely shattered. It's not just the one day's labour. It's the unending labour of a hundred days, a thousand days. He's grateful for the work, but it's killing him. Then he remembers the pills Stevie sold him in the pub a couple of nights ago. He doesn't know exactly what they are: 'Man, ye can gan forever on these' was how Stevie made his pitch. Amphetamines, Benzedrine, Mephedrone – who cares? As long as they sort him out.

They do something to him, that's for sure. Half an hour after taking them he feels less tired; but also a whole lot worse, as if something has changed inside him, or something outside has changed, but he's not sure what.

Maybe it's the pills, maybe not. As dusk approaches, his sense of unease grows. All his life Geordie has worked alone. He's used to being in the middle of nowhere. This *is* the middle of nowhere: a remote area of the forest between Kershope Rigg and Blacklyne Common. Walkers and farmers rarely come here. There is no reason to: no grazing, no paths that go anywhere, nothing to see except trees. There's nobody here; not at this time of day. He has heard the barking of foxes, the alarm calls of birds and often he has heard the screams of buzzards overhead as they float sideways in the winds that never stop blowing across these Border hills.

Now all he hears is the silence, and it is getting on his nerves. When the trailer has been loaded and the huge stack of wooden poles secured, he climbs into the cab of the big Scania and turns the key in the ignition.

He knows that the pills have done something weird to him. He wishes he hadn't taken them, but it's too late for that. His heart is pounding much too fast and he can feel the sweat beading on his forehead. He flicks on the headlights as he enters the dark tunnel of trees, following the intricate and confusing maze of forest roads down into the valley of the North Tyne, to Leaplish and on down to the chipboard factory in Hexham to drop off his load. When he's done that he will drive to the village beside the Tyne where Mary and he live in their flat. There's something else getting into his head: something he thinks he has seen rather than heard.

He switches on some music to drown out these odd and unwelcome thoughts – not really thoughts, but flashes from somewhere arriving in his brain like radio signals. Then the huge truck meets blacktop road, and he pushes the accelerator to the floor. Headlamps on full beam, the trailer sways dangerously as he drives much too fast down the valley. Only when the lights of the first villages appear does he slow down a little. As he drives through them, images come to him: images of children. In many of the houses, lights glow from upstairs windows. He imagines that those lights are illuminating bathrooms and bedrooms. He imagines children at their bath-time; children having stories read to them by their parents, sitting on the side of the bed, turning the pages in the gentle glow of a bedside lamp. He imagines the children turning over sleepily in bed and murmuring goodnight. He imagines – so clearly – the father and the mother smiling at each other as they close the door softly on the sleeping child. He imagines it; he remembers it.

Mary is watching television when he arrives home. She stands up as he comes through the door, but does not offer him a kiss or greet him in any way. Instead she puts the kettle on. She knows he won't eat straightaway. He is too tired to eat, almost too tired to speak. He accepts a mug of tea from her and asks how she is.

'All right.'

A little later, he stands up, as if uncertain what to do next. Mary asks: 'Will I get you something to eat?'

'No – I'll do myself a fry-up in the morning.'

She leaves the room. He hears her running the tap in the bathroom and then the door of her room shuts. It isn't really her bedroom. It used to be the nursery, where the boy slept. He disappeared just before Christmas, when most buildings in the street had fairy lights hanging over the door and Christmas trees visible through the windows. He disappeared while they were starting to wrap his Christmas presents, while Christmas carols played incessantly on the radio and Christmas jingles played over the public address systems in the supermarkets.

That was four months ago, and more. Mary hasn't changed anything. The toys are all still in the cupboards. The ceiling is still pasted with stars and crescent moons that glow a little in the dark when the lights are switched off. Mary moved in there a few weeks after the boy went. She and Geordie haven't shared a bed since. They haven't shared much else either: not their thoughts, nor their worries. They have plenty of those, but they no longer talk about them.

It's one of those things. She doesn't particularly blame Geordie for what happened; that's to say, she blames him equally along with the rest of the human race.

An hour or two later, Geordie switches off the television. He has no idea what he has been watching. He goes to the bathroom and brushes his teeth. He goes to their bedroom and strips off to his boxer shorts and climbs into bed. He sleeps in the middle now; it's less lonely. After a few minutes he falls asleep, but it is not the dreamless sleep of the tired man. His hands twitch and he moans once or twice. Then he mutters to himself: '*Light in the forest. Light in the forest.*'

There is no one to hear him, and when he wakes in the morning he doesn't remember his dreams. There is no one beside him to ask how he slept, or nuzzle against him for a moment before he steps out of bed. He showers, then dresses laboriously, for the tiredness from the day before hasn't left him. He goes into the kitchen and puts on the kettle. He raps gently on Mary's door to see if she wants a cup of tea bringing in. There is no answer. They still love each other, he tells himself, although it's hard to say why, or how you would know, they see so little of one another these days. He cooks himself a good breakfast: two fried eggs, beans, tinned tomatoes, bacon, a mug of hot tea with two sugars. After he has eaten, he experiences a rush as the glucose and the fats surge into his bloodstream – an illusion of energy; an illusion of purpose. By the time he has climbed into the truck and started it up, that flicker has died down again and he already feels weary as he heads north, back towards the forest.

Also by *Sunday Times* bestseller Paul Torday:

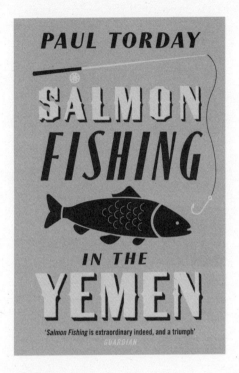

PAUL TORDAY

SALMON FISHING IN THE YEMEN

'*Salmon Fishing* is extraordinary indeed, and a triumph'
GUARDIAN

'An entertaining and successful debut . . . feel-good
comedy with surprising bite' *Sunday Telegraph*

When he is asked to become involved in a project to
create a salmon river in the highlands of the Yemen,
fisheries scientist Dr Alfred Jones rejects the idea as
absurd. But the proposal catches the eye of several
senior British politicians. And so Fred finds himself
forced to set aside his research and instead figure out
how to fly ten thousand salmon to a desert country –
and persuade them to swim there . . .

As he embarks on an extraordinary journey of faith, the diffident Dr Jones will discover a sense of belief, and a capacity for love, that surprises himself and all who know him.

'A stunning debut' *Daily Mail*

'*Salmon Fishing* is extraordinary indeed, and a triumph' *Guardian*

WINNER OF THE BOLLINGER EVERYMAN WODEHOUSE PRIZE FOR COMIC FICTION

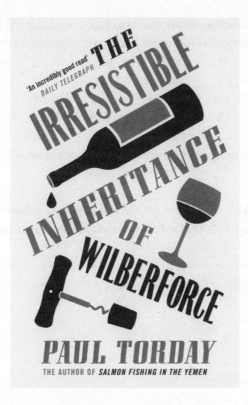

'An incredibly good read'
DAILY TELEGRAPH

'Exceptionally accomplished . . . Torday has managed a near masterpiece' *Daily Express*

Late one summer evening, Wilberforce – rich, young, and work-obsessed – makes a detour on his way home to the vast undercroft of Caerlyon Hall, and the domain of Francis Black, a place where wine, hospitality and affection flow freely.

Through Francis, Wilberforce is initiated into a life rich in the promise of friendship and adventure, where, through his new set of friends, the possibility of finding acceptance and even falling in love, seems finally to be within his reach.

In the cellars of Caerlyon, Wilberforce nurtures a new-found passion for wine. But even the finest wine can leave a bitter aftertaste and Wilberforce will learn the undercroft's unpalatable secrets and that passion comes at a price . . .

'The whole book is delightfully written . . . Paul Torday is a remarkably original novelist' *Evening Standard*

'Grows more and more poignant as the novel progresses . . . satisfyingly full-bodied and slips down a treat' *Sunday Times*

'A clever, gripping novel'
THE TIMES

THE

GIRL

ON THE

LANDING

PAUL TORDAY

AUTHOR OF *SALMON FISHING IN THE YEMEN*

'This is an exciting novel – part love story, part psycho-logical thriller – which confounds your expectations as it tightens its grip' *Mail on Sunday*

Michael is dressing for dinner at a friend's country house in Ireland. As he descends the staircase, he admires a small painting of a landing. In the background is a woman clad in a dark green dress. During dinner, Michael comments on the painting to his hosts but they say there is no woman in the picture. When Michael goes up to bed later, he sees that they are correct.

This is only the first in a series of incidents that lead Michael to question his grip on reality. His wife Elizabeth is unsettled by the changes she sees in a man she originally married because he was dependable and steady, not because she loved him. She realises she has never really known Michael and as he changes, she sees glimpses of someone she could fall in love with . . .

'The best book of the year . . . a truly astonishing take on what appears on the surface to be mental illness and turns out to be something far darker' *Sunday Express*

'The story of Michael Gascoigne's strange affinity with the wilderness unravels slowly, tantalisingly' *Guardian*